I0450882

# Carved In Stone
## A Monsters Of Crossgate Novel

## Sabrina Blackburry

Copyright © 2025 by Sabrina Blackburry

All rights reserved.

**Content warning:** sex, language, violence, kidnapping, fear of heights, parental loss, estranged/low-contact family.

No portion of this book may be reproduced in any form without written permission from the publisher or author, except as permitted by U.S. copyright law.

Names, characters, places, and incidents featured in this publication are either the product of the author's imagination or are used fictitiously. Any resemblance to actual persons (living or dead), events, institutions, or locales, without satiric intent, is coincidental.

NO AI TRAINING: Without in any way limiting the author's exclusive rights under copyright, any use of this publication to "train" generative artificial intelligence (AI) technologies to generate text is expressly prohibited. The author reserves all rights to license uses of this work for generative AI training and development of machine learning language models.

Cover Design by KitFoxArt

Editing by Ashley Wessel

Formatting by Lashell Rain

This book is dedicated to Keith David.
He knows what he did.

# Chapter One

## Zendrax

**The realm of Stone Wings, the plateau above Stoneforge Castle**

When the moon's embrace woke me this night, surrounded by the sounds of battle and blood, I did not think it would be my last. I certainly did not believe it would be at the hands of my uncle. But Havaxus stood over me, expression grim as he spoke the ancient words of disgrace.

"Zendrax, son of Tava, warrior of Stoneforge." My uncle hesitated, then sighed. "You dare to live when your clan has fallen. You live when your matron has died, your sisters have died, and you have failed in your familial duties to protect Stoneforge Castle."

The dark sky was simmering with the red of an impending sunrise that would sweep away the dust of the battlefield. The crumbled stone corpses of my clan lay in the ruins alongside the

1

human queen's army, also decimated and broken in the wake of the enemy army that took us by surprise.

A roar tore from my chest. A lament for the lost, for my kin and kind, for the fallen human court whose queen I had called friend. My clan once thrived in our duty atop the spires and walls of Stoneforge, watching vigilantly for danger; until now. And it had broken me. The tear in my left wing would heal, the cracked talons at my feet would regrow, and the deep jabs of arrows that peppered my shoulder blade would mend. But my heart would forever be torn. My family and clan were now lost, and any who could have helped piece together how it happened so swiftly, with no warning, were now dead and crumbled. On my knees, the red clay of the plateau high above Stoneforge Castle sank into my skin, covering the lacerations of battle and burning in my blood.

It was no choice at all. Death would honor my failure, and exile would only prolong it. Wandering the Dusts with no kin and clan for what, decades more? The beasts of the wilderness would devour me, the sun's wrath would crumble me, the loneliness would smother me. In death, there was at least some small honor.

"End me," I demanded, my voice cracking with torment. I would not live with this failure.

"Are you certain, nephew?" Havaxus stood tall over me, his broad shoulders the same pale granite as my mother's. I could have claimed the same if not for the thin veins of jade that threaded through my wings, a reminder of my father. Havaxus and his clan, a sister to our own, watched over the Grand Gate on the far side of the gorge. My uncle arrived with his warriors, but not before our leader, my mother, had fallen. It wrenched my stomach that he would have the burden of my unmaking, and right after witnessing the crumbled form of his twin.

"Zendrax!" my cousin exclaimed, "Give your answer due consideration, I beg of you." My injuries throbbed. The laceration across my wing ached worst of all. The gaping wound clouded my head, even through the grief. But my eyes still focused on his form in the crowd of pained gargoyles. We had grown up together, often spending weeks at a time visiting and training. If I were to have a brother, it would have been Nyzax. My eyes roamed over him for the last time. He was on track to grow even larger than his father. He was capable, ambitious. My younger cousin would be a powerful leader. Everything the clans would need; once I was gone.

"I am sorry, Zax," I murmured. He scowled and looked to the ground, unable to face me. I understood. Turning back to Havaxus, I bowed my head.

"I have no remaining words, Uncle." My voice was rough with emotion. The loss of my mother and sisters hadn't fully consumed me, but the monstrous grief that sat on my shoulders would devour me if I lived on. At least this way I could die with dignity.

Havaxus raised his head, and closing his eyes, he declared, "So be it."

"Wait!" someone in the crowd called, parting the mass of bodies and wings.

I grunted, frustrated. They were delaying my death. To what end? No amount of arguing was going to stop this from happening, and so I'd rather get it done with.

"What is it, Marzav?" Havaxus asked, warily.

An aged gargoyle. One of the surviving elders of my clan, respected and wise. His movements were slower than my memory from childhood as he stepped forward to speak. His survival of the battle came as a surprise, and my eyes slid to the horizon. We needed to end this soon so the remaining clan could find some place safe to turn stone before the approaching daylight. But he was an elder, and we owed him our attentions, even at this urgent time.

Marzav made his way to Havaxus's side, his ancient eyes settling on me for a long, strained moment before he spoke. "Zendrax, you are the pride and joy your mother left behind. She did not fail us, she fought for us. Your sisters fought for us. Your survival of this battle does not negate the fact that every one of us saw you fight for us as well."

Agreement rippled through the gathered clans, and a few shouted their own accounts of what they saw. Such a mix of grief and pain did not leave room for my heart to hold anything else, and instead of taking pride in my deeds, I only found myself numb to their words.

"Still," I countered, "I did not fall, and the queen's rule has ended. I have failed these lands as surely as I have broken the promise of my lineage to watch over Stoneforge."

"Then leave these lands," Marzav said. "Live, youngling. These old eyes have not witnessed a more noble soul than the children of Tava. Exile indeed is a lonely pursuit, but I propose to you the ancient right of banishment from the realm. Build yourself a new life, Zendrax. I would see the child of Tava repent with good deeds. I would see you sow the seeds of hope and honor away from the reminders of this past."

"Hear, hear!" a few shouted.

Havaxus looked at Marzav, then to me. "The right of banishment . . . The ways of magic have been long lost to the humans. We no longer have a means to open such a portal."

"I do," Marzav said simply, letting the shock settle over the crowd.

"What law do you speak of?" I demanded. "I will not shame myself or my family line by running away." My shoulders heaved as my wings spread involuntarily, sweeping away from me as though I would attack. The pull of my heart in many directions threatened to overwhelm me. Fear, distress, hope, heartache, all wrapped into one moment. Death would be an honorable grace. What penance could I serve in another realm?

"I say that the old ways would see you live, Zendrax." Marzav walked the few steps to close the distance, placing his hand on my brow between my horns. "The old ways demanded only the death of the failed clan leader, never the blood of their children.

We may give the choice of death or exile, but there was once another way to handle this and I have not forgotten it."

"I have never heard of a disgraced line choosing the shame of exile," my cousin spoke up, unsure. "Are you saying there's a way for Zendrax to live? And it is not to wander the Dusts?"

This time, it was Havaxus who answered. "Marzav speaks true. The old ways would banish the remainder of the family to another realm, to live the rest of their lives seeking to do good and repent for the failures of their line. Once the humans we protect lost their magic, we could no longer banish them as we once had. Instead, our kind began to crumble the family, or cast them away from the clans in exile to the Dusts."

My eyes sharpened on the elder gargoyle. "What portals do you speak of? Our kind do not use magic. There is no way for this banishment. Please, spare me the heartache and let me die on the field my family has sworn to look after so that our clans may seek refuge from the daylight!"

"Please," Marzav asked, "for Tava."

My throat tightened at the mention of my mother. Looking to the edge of the plateau, as if I could see over it and down to the castle where her crumbled form lay at the gate where she fell. Marzav wasn't the only one to beg, as the words of people I had known my whole life floated around the crowd. I could not form the words, but I finally nodded my approval.

Havaxus looked to his people, to the remainder of my people, and heaved a sigh. "Nyzax, take everyone from this place and stone in the forest for the day. I will stay with Marzav and

Zendrax, and upon my return, my nephew will either be banished or . . ."

The words fell away, but everyone knew what he meant. If Marzav's plan to banish me failed, my uncle would have to shatter my heart and crumble my body.

Nyzax had an unreadable expression, worry and pain swirling in his eyes. He looked to me for a moment, opening his mouth as though he would speak before snapping it shut again. He turned to his father next. "I will do as you say."

Lifting into the air, a chorus of wingbeats followed him. My heart eased, knowing Nyzax would care for everyone today. Knowing the humans that now dwelled in Stoneforge Castle would be too busy bringing everyone to order reassured me they likely wouldn't have time to hunt down the rest of the gargoyles. I watched as they flew away to the forest, where dark branches and tall trees would keep them safe.

"Alright, Marzav," Uncle said softly, "tell us your plans."

The old gargoyle nodded and turned to point toward the gorge. "Do you remember the castle scholar who was translating the scrolls from the old library wing?"

Since he was not from this land, Havaxus looked to me for the answer. I nodded. The grizzled human spent his last decades on those scrolls.

Marzav continued, "There is a cave in which he painted some summoning rings he had found. I helped carry him and his supplies myself. We found a safe place that could harm no spectators if something went wrong. Most of the scrolls were completely useless without magic, of course, but one of them supposedly called for a demon to come. A demon of portals from another world."

Stunned, I looked from the old gargoyle to my uncle.

"And you're certain this demon could take Zendrax? We could spare his life?" Havaxus asked.

"There is only one way to find out," Marzav said. "I will take you to the cave, but we will need spirits and smoking herbs to summon the demon. The translations were difficult, remnants of old research, but I believe I can find both in the cave itself."

Havaxus nodded, his body already moving stiffly as he gazed towards the rapidly approaching sun. "Then we move now. Perhaps we can hold off turning to stone until after we see Zendrax off."

My heart beat fiercely in my chest, stone to bones. I still did not know if I even wanted to survive, but maybe an exile would be best. To spend my days mourning and trying to make amends for the failures of my kin.

"Very well," I said, finally rising from my knees. "I will do whatever you command, Uncle."

Within the high walls of the gorge, we indeed found a cave that nearly blended in. Despite having grown up gliding over the gorge, I had never seen the place Marzav brought us to. I could see the stiffness, the struggle in my uncle's shoulders fending off the call of the sun to turn to stone and rest. The aged gargoyle was even stiffer with the struggle. I could feel it, the call to stone and recover my injuries, but I would resist it until my body crumbled to dust if it meant relieving my uncle of the burden of my death at his hands. I could only pray that Marzav was right.

The cave was dusty, coated in a layer of the red gorge's dirt blown in by the wind. But it had indeed been the workplace of a researcher. Long ago, someone collected many of the books and scrolls, taking them back to the castle for proper storage. But the remnants of mystical markings graced the walls and floors, as well as the weathered desks and benches where the scholar conducted his research.

Walking through the cool cavernous space, I ran a clawed finger along one of the painted wall runes. "How does this work, exactly?"

"We place our offering at the correct place and light a candle," Marzav answered.

"That's it?" Havaxus asked.

"Yes. The process is simple, according to the texts. Whether this demon responds or not is up to them." Marzav took a pouch of smoking herbs and a bottle of dark liquid with the wax seal still intact and began studying the runes. On the ground, round markings cut sections of the floor while other strange shapes graced the walls. But I followed him, my uncle at my side, until Marzav brought us to a smooth part of the wall with a red painted grand arch design.

We watched, mesmerized, as Marzav set the bottle and the pouch in two empty circles on the floor where the painted design crossed from wall to ground in just enough space to make what looked like a doorstep in the paint. At each bottom corner, he lit a candle, and once he was done, he stood back and waited.

"Now what?" Havaxus asked.

"Now, we hope that the demon answers our call." The old gargoyle's voice was rough, strained. "Before one or all of us stone for the day."

The silence of the cavern was somber. Reflective. The wind howled outside the entrance, but the three of us were still.

After what felt like much longer than it probably was, the candles flickered. At first, the flames danced in the motionless air of the cave. Unsettling in their unnatural movements. I shared a look with my uncle, but when we turned to Marzav, his hands and feet were already turning to stone.

"Marzav—" I began.

"Hush," he said, simply. "Tava was the heart of the clan. I will see her son safely away; repentance or not."

The candles suddenly snuffed out, leaving us in the dark space with only the scent of smoke and a sense of high alert, until the painted archway began to glow. The red glimmer was disturbing, an unnatural light coming from it as the space within the arch swirled, ivory white mixed with red smoke until red consumed the whole thing.

"Magic," Havaxus hissed.

From the smoke stepped a demon. I hadn't seen one before, but from the old artworks and ancient texts, this creature could be nothing else. Skin of living ivory and hair to match, eyes like burning red coals. The demon stepped forward and looked between the three of us. What emerged was a feminine figure, in a shirt of buttons that were mostly undone, with a pair of black pants in a style unfamiliar to this realm. The demon was nothing like I'd seen before. She stooped down to pick up the offerings of the bottle and the pouch.

She murmured to herself in another language, but her tone was appreciative as she pulled free a pipe from within her strange shirt and stuffed it with the offered smoking herbs. Lighting it with what appeared to be sparks from her fingers, she didn't pay us any attention until she had puffed the first breath from her pipe.

She spoke again in that language, then slowly sized each of us up.

"Madam, we cannot understand your words," Marzav said.

She paused, looking bored as she puffed at her pipe. But with a snap of her fingers, something popped in my ears. It startled me, and from his body language, it startled my uncle as well.

"There," she said, "try again."

I didn't like this. This demon was powerful, with unknown magics. But Marzav continued. "Please, demon of portals. I have begged your attention in this place so that we can ask that you take Zendrax, son of Tava of the Stoneforge Clan, to another realm where he may be banished and repent."

Her gaze moved from the old gargoyle to me, contemplative, as she tucked the unopened bottle of spirits under one arm. "And what would you bargain for me to take him?"

I snarled. The insinuation that she would require more from my people than they had already provided churned badly in my stomach. "You will ask nothing from them, as I am the one who must pay this price."

"Zen—" Havaxus began.

"No, Uncle," I told him, and then turned to the demon. "Please, what task may I owe you in return? What foe may I slay, or treasure may I find you? Please."

The demon smiled, her glowing coal eyes narrowing. "Well, I suppose it's not a difficult thing. And you did pique my interest with your offerings. Fine, you will owe me a favor, and I will take you with me to my realm."

My heart stilled. It was really going to happen. I was going to leave this place. My clan, the skies I've always flown and the walls I've always guarded. I turned to my uncle and Marzav.

"Go, Zendrax," Marzav said, smiling even as his arms began to turn. He saw to it that his plan was a success, and now he could fight the day no more. "Live well and do good. For us."

"Marzav," I choked as he finished turning.

"Zen," my uncle drew my attention, and even his claws were beginning to turn to stone. "Be well, my nephew. Repent for Tava and live a long life in your new realm."

"Come, gargoyle," the demon said. With one last look at my uncle, I nodded. There were no more words to be had between us, but I hoped the look I gave him could convey everything I wanted him to know.

Turning to the demon, I took her outstretched hand, and through the smoke and portal we went.

Away from this realm for good.

# Chapter Two

## Henri

**Crossgate City**

"God fucking shit, piece of fuck rock!" My little toe throbbed as I lifted my foot to grab it with both hands, putting pressure on the area that I just stubbed on a sizeable chunk of granite.

My studio was usually full of rocks. But this one in particular I picked up a while back and still didn't know what I was going to make out of it. Seeing as how this was the third time I'd stubbed my toes on it in the month I'd had it, I felt tempted to make it into a pile of rubble instead of a sculpture. But it was an expensive chunk of material, and I wasn't about to carve it until I had the perfect plan for it. My attention slid to the fridge, where I'd hung the colorful poster for the centennial celebration public art instillation contest. The prize money would be sweet, and the victory to rub in my family's face—even sweeter.

When my toe finally stopped throbbing, I rubbed my eyes and glowered at the dusty apartment. An attic, really, of one of the gothic buildings in Old Town where the architecture was interesting, and the nights were long and lively. I could get lost in my art and still go around the block for shrimp fried rice at one in the morning if I felt like it. Sure, it was a crappy attic with a finicky shower. I had to throw sheets on my furniture to protect it from stone dust while I worked despite the room dividers and plastic curtains I'd hung, and there were no laundry hookups so I had to walk it to the first floor and pay for coin-operated laundry, but it was mine. Where else was I going to find somewhere to live and work with a freight elevator accessible? The building was once a factory of some kind—shoes or something—and all it took for me to sign the lease was the assurance that a few chunks of rock here and there wouldn't be a problem with the floors. Besides, I could only handle sixty pounds or so on my own, so unless I wanted to hire movers, I rarely brought in something large. Except for the stupid piece of granite that I kept running into with my foot. That was going to be a pain to get out of here once I was done.

Taking in the undeniable mess around me, I winced at the debris and supplies I'd allowed to stray from the protective canvas tarps on the floor. A mess of dishes teetered in the sink, punctuated by an empty pizza box. Pizza that I couldn't even remember ordering. I recognized the need for some fresh air before I knew I would need to come back and clean up the aftermath of a week-long sculpting spree.

Turning my back to the workspace, I stretched my arms high, passing by the kitchenette counter where I'd thrown my mail earlier that day. A thick envelope that I'd ignored stood out from the rest. Sighing through my nose and already knowing what I'd find in it, I opened the letter to see yet another job application to a bottom-rung position in one of my parents' country club friends' businesses. I threw it at the trash can, cursing as it slipped off the top of the heaping pile and onto the floor.

"Fucking hell, Henri. When are you going to get it together?" I mumbled to myself; a habit that had only gotten worse since living alone. *That's it,* I thought. *I need to leave this apartment for a while.* I picked the letter back up, then shoved it into the trashcan, using it to press the rest of the junk down with it. Storming over to my nightstand, I scrounged around for a scrunchie to pull the mass of loose orange curls out of my face. Then I took a swipe of chapstick across my lips before piling my hair up in some kind of ball on top of my head.

Grabbing my sketchbook, I padded across the apartment on bare feet, wearing nothing but an oversized t-shirt from the pizza place I'd worked at in high school and my favorite pair of black lace panties. Quite the combination, and I considered putting on actual pants, but the summer was still winding down its heat and no one was going to see me on the roof so high off the street. The no-pants club won out, and I opened the squeaky hinges of the gorgeous windows to step out onto the ledge, bare legs and all.

Out on the roof, it was a wide enough space for someone to walk cautiously. The path had a low iron fencing that trimmed it, though, only being a foot or so tall, it wouldn't stop a determined tumble off the roof. I had already been out here a dozen times since moving in. This part was a bit scary, but just around the corner was a wide space with a low slope that climbed all the way up to the flattened top, perfect for admiring the sunset and sketching the stone carvings that had drawn me to move here in the first place.

Settling down on the safe part of the roof, I looked around at the carved corners, tall pillars, and gargoyles of the Gothic District around me. Lights were coming on as the pink-tinged sky began its blaze down to the horizon where it would dip away, revealing the streetlights and neon signs below.

Pencil in hand, I flipped to a clean page as my eye caught a large gargoyle near the far side of the roof. I hadn't drawn it before. In fact, I couldn't remember looking at it at all. Setting my supplies down, I crawled the low slope on my hands and knees until I could see it up close. A huge gargoyle, wings cradling its back as though it wanted to hide away from the world. Something about it made me sad. Crawling further around, I got a look at its face and sucked in a breath.

The heartbreak and resolve on its face were breathtaking. Whoever had carved it was a master of their craft. Its features were so sharp, almost alive in their detail. The jawline was strong, and I could almost reach up and trace the sinew that ran there. The arms were an impressive study of muscle structure, and the wings were fine, like bat wings, so thin that they let a hint of light shine through them as the last rays of the sun slipped away.

I had to get closer. It was sitting on the roof where I felt safest, but the flat ledge that ran all the way around the roof with its little safety trim made room for me to get in front of the gorgeous piece of stone.

I crawled, fat ass in the air, as I went down the low slope of the roof and settled myself before the gargoyle. It was beautiful from all angles, the afterglow of the sleeping sun now casting shadows across the ridges. It was striking. Ethereal, haunting, grounded. So many things all at once. The shape of the neck drew me, so did the round of the shoulders. My eyes traced the face, the chest, the remarkable detail down the stomach, the . . . I snorted. This thing had an impressive cock. I would envy the lady gargoyles, but that thing would break a human in half.

Still, I loved the shape of it. Thicker in the middle, with a soft round form to the head that looked so real and inviting. I nibbled at my bottom lip while studying it.

I shrugged, committing to my curiosity. *It's about the only thing I can reach from this part of the roof, anyway.*

Reaching out a hand, I let my fingers brush down the length of it. It was so smooth, a silky texture for stone that must have taken a long time to perfect. I wanted another feel. This time I placed my entire palm on it, slowly moving downward on the sun-warmed stone.

And it twitched.

I yelped and jumped back, so startled by the impossible movement of the statue that I lost my footing completely. With a shriek, I flailed my arms to no avail as my weight tipped back too far to recover. Doom sank into me as I began to fall backward, over the pathetic iron details that would in no way save my ass from the six-story drop.

Something rough grabbed my leg and my whole body jerked at a change in direction. My heart drummed in my chest as I felt myself dangling by an ankle as a face full of open air high over a busy street below shot fear through me. And then, I felt my body turn to face the roof.

The gargoyle was holding me by the ankle like I weighed nothing. He spread his wings out behind him for balance, and his head tilted as he stared at me inquisitively with jade eyes.

"Greetings," he rumbled in a low voice.

I giggled. Not the giggle from before, when I saw his cock, but a panicked bubbling sound that stressed just how close I was to snapping from shock.

He pulled me close to him, moving me until I was upright and facing him. He had a hand under each of my arms, holding me out like I would hold my baby cousin, and pulled me closer to see.

"I am Zendrax."

I screamed. A reasonable enough reaction, in my opinion, as I didn't wake up this morning expecting to talk to a statue. Was this technically a statue? By the definition of the word, I suppose not.

"Why do you scream?" he asked. "I saved you."

Wriggling in his grasp, I was pushing and pulling against the immoveable hands that kept me in place. "Put me down!"

The rock—*Zendrax*—paused to consider my words before standing up from his squatting position and then walked us across the roof.

"Where are we go—DO NOT DROP ME! Are you listening?" I went from trying to pry myself out of his hands to holding onto them for dear life. I wasn't particularly afraid of heights before this, but there was a good chance of a new trauma surfacing to ensure I had a healthy dose of respect for rooftops from now on.

I'll be the first to admit my imagination has always allowed me to believe in the supernatural. Ghosts and aliens and vampires and everything else were on the table, as far as I'm concerned. But seeing something in the flesh was quite a different matter. The gargoyle was huge, now that he was standing upright, at close to seven feet tall. Taking in his horns and wings, I added a few more inches to my estimation.

He looked around until he found the window I had climbed out of and stepped us inside. He had to stoop low to fit, and as soon as he was on stable ground, he placed me on my feet. My legs were shaking so hard I let myself sink to the rug I kept by the large windows, thankful for whatever cushion it could give me.

A gargoyle was in my apartment, and it was walking around. Or, more accurately, he was barely through the window bay when he offered a nod and began to turn around. A million thoughts crossed my mind in a heartbeat. *What the fuck is going on*, was at the top of that list. Other thoughts that followed were things like: *How is he walking? Why is he naked? Where did he come from? Am I hallucinating?* But before I could finish letting the wild thoughts run their course, those beautiful wings, more captivating now that they were moving right in front of me, turned as he made to leave through the window.

"Wait," the words left my mouth, a soft and curious plea.

Wait?

*Wait?*

What was I saying?

I reached out, possibly acting on instinct as my fingers wrapped around the part of him closest to me, his tail. It slid out of my loose grip as he turned, now facing me with suspicion. Or maybe it was caution.

My hand still felt the ghost of his touch in my palm. His tail was hard but smooth, and if I had to guess from the seconds I had contact with him, I would say there was a minute amount of give to the firm surface. He wasn't quite solid, though plenty close to it. But the touch of my hand on him when I thought he was a statue was far harder, the stone I had expected to feel under my fingertips.

Oh god, I'd touched a lot more than just his skin. A flush hit my face. Closing my fingers over my palm, as I remembered what exactly it was that I had been stroking when he came to life and startled me. I moved my attention back to him, trying to shove away the embarrassment even as my curiosity burned to learn more. "How is it that you're moving?"

Living stone, Zendrax was swift and silent as a cat, despite his considerable size and whatever weight that amount of stone added up to. His jade eyes practically glowed in the moonlight that flooded in from the window beside us.

"I am alive." He furrowed his brow. "I move for the same reason you do."

"No, I mean, am I dreaming right now?" I asked. It was a stupid question. If I was dreaming, he wouldn't tell me, would he? Shaking my head, a few orange coils pulled loose and bounced at the side of my vision before I tucked them away. Zendrax tracked the movement with keen interest. "But what are you? I want to know everything."

He paused, considering my words carefully. I took the time to look at his details closer. His hair, could you call it hair? Was it soft or hard? It looked smooth as it swept down his head and settled around the base of his skull. When his mouth moved, were those . . . fangs? Or just pointy teeth, perhaps. He was so beautiful. Not a word I used lightly on living things instead of art, but here he was, and I had no better word for him.

"You wish to . . . know me?" he asked.

The tone in which he asked was heartbreaking, and it made me wonder why. What happened to this creature? What brought him to the roof and left him so somber and resolved?

My voice came out raspy, barely audible above the city streets below, with the cars and the people. But I was sure when I said it, and Zendrax heard me loud and clear. "Yeah."

# Chapter Three

## Zendrax

Her dark topaz eyes were bright, like the lights of the city below. Full of curiosity, this human, but not of fear as I had expected. The Mistress said the people here do not know my kind, of any kinds other than their own, and that I should stay hidden from them. Tiny brown stars speckled the skin across her face and traced down her arms. Her hair, made of swirling strands of sunset, gently framed her face. The garment she wore did not seem timely for the cool night air, or at least the other humans I'd observed were wearing fabrics on their legs, unlike this one, who had on a large tunic and nothing else.

My mouth nearly twitched up at the corner. I couldn't say she had nothing else when I observed the black undergarment when I caught her by the ankle. Woven threads in patterns of flowers, surely not meant for heavy use for fear they would fall apart.

"I'm Henri," she said. "How did you get on the roof?"

What a complicated question that was, one I'd spent the past few months reflecting on. I awaited word from The Mistress regarding my repayment for transportation to this realm and reflecting on the battle which determined my fate. My time was to be spent on repentance and doing good in my clan's name, but that wasn't easy when you weren't to reveal yourself to the general population. Not that it mattered now, but I supposed I'd done one good deed in saving this human, Henri. But in the process, I did not do as I'd been told in this foreign land where I did not understand the rules yet.

Moving uncomfortably, watching that my wings did not scrape the ceiling, I tried not to catch the claws of my feet on the soft rug. "I flew up there."

Henri laughed, a bubbly, warm sound that struck me as comfortable. Had I been away from others for so long that a simple laugh was this enjoyable? Perhaps.

"Flying, obviously. Surely those giant wings aren't just for show. I mean, how did you come to be there in the first place?" She frowned. "I always thought it would be cool to meet a cryptid or something, but after seeing just how real it is to stand in front of one . . . Damn, I hope the other things I'm imagining aren't real. That would be terrifying."

Whatever else she could imagine being fearful of had me clenching my teeth. This roof was now claimed by a gargoyle, though a fallen one, and there was no threat in this realm that I would not defend this building from. I lost many things from my realm. My family, my clan, my home, but in the months of life in this city, I have laid claim to the buildings of this block, and under my watch they will remain until the day I crumble.

"That won't be a problem," I responded. "No one will come to harm beneath my rooftop."

I'd answered so quickly that I surprised myself. They were easy words, said often in my homeland and layered with the bonds of trust, loyalty, and guardianship established by my ancestors and carried through my clan's history. Until me, that is.

"Oh," she said as her eyes stretched open just a bit wider, moving to the claws at my fingertips. "So, you've always been on this roof? Your whole life?"

"No." It came out colder than I had intended, so I softened my tone. "No, I'm from another realm."

My words did not deter the human. She spilled over with more curiosity, tilting her head in a way that bounced her sunset curls around her shoulders. "How did you get here? What do you mean by 'other realm?' What do you eat? I hope it's not people. Can I draw you?"

"I'm not sure, a sort of magic perhaps. Another realm, both like and unlike this one. There were tall towers, wide landscapes, a crest of the sun and rise of the moons in turn."

"Moons, like two of them?" She clapped her hands together in front of her chin. "Can I draw you, please?"

It was the second time she had asked that. "You wish to capture my appearance in an art form?"

"In charcoal, yes." She turned to a large table, taking up much of the room and cluttered with a number of things, pulling free a bound book of paper and flipping it open. "I'm an artist, a sculptor when I can afford the materials. I draw and paint, too. My favorite subjects are architectural design."

The pages turned one by one, revealing details that most would pass by on the street without notice. Not Henri, she had taken the time to capture a corner of crown molding, an arched window set in stone and stained glass, the roofline I recognized from the building next to this one, a view she had from the very window we stood in front of now.

I was mesmerized. Of course, there were grand artists in Stoneforge, but I spent little time around them. The lumbering shape of gargoyles was ill-suited to an art studio, and I would rather spend my time outside hunting, playing games of skill with my clanmates, teaching the fledglings, and watching over the land than indoors. I had always known humans to be creative, but the beauty of what this little human could create with her hands was fascinating. With their soft bodies, they can make art and music, and dance with grace, or sing like a bird if they practiced their craft. Henri, it would seem, was no exception.

"You are skilled," I murmured, taking the book from her with gentle hands and flipping the page. A grand column, and a part of a carved doorway.

"Thanks, if only my mother felt the same way." She tried to shrug off the compliment, but the skin across her nose and cheeks blushed, adding a pink haze beneath the sea of brown stars on her face.

Taking my time to study a few more pages, I closed the book gently and handed it back to her. What would it mean for me to agree to her request? Surely, the act of sitting still was no match for a gargoyle, but there were other obligations I had in this place. The Mistress was clear with her rules, and on this night, I broke one of them when I revealed myself to Henri. But this human's open curiosity and conversation was the most alive I'd felt in weeks. The Mistress had invited me to spend as much time as I wished in her personal establishment. A tavern of sorts, or whatever version of an alehouse that existed in this realm. A place where others like me could coexist, creatures unknown to this human world that had to hide and conceal themselves to be here. Though the offer was well intentioned, or at least uninhibited by a demon's bargain, I could not find any moments of peace or comfort in that place. The atmosphere of merriment, boldness, and lust was not in line with my repentance. This apartment, however, was a warm breath of rest for a weary soul. The rooftops in this part of the city were more familiar, reminiscent of Stoneforge. A quiet place to find refuge for a lone gargoyle. Whatever I had to do to make things right with the demoness and still get to know Henri, I would do it. If I must, I would resort to another bargain.

"I would be honored for you to draw me." And I meant it. This was the most time I had spent with anyone since coming to this place. There was something comforting about Henri that allowed me to indulge, despite my banishment, in a moment of enjoyment.

"Yes!" Henri said, bouncing on the balls of her feet and raising her arms in the air until she realized those black threads that she called undergarments flashed on full display.

"Whoops." She pulled the hem of her shirt down. "Shit, sorry. The second I'm home, I'm a member of the no-pants club."

"I'm not familiar with the organization," I admitted.

"Nevermind," she laughed. "Alright, so I'd like to pick up some more charcoal and a bigger board for this. Can I see you tomorrow?"

A deal was to be struck with this artist made of stars and sunset. My knowledge of this realm may be lacking, but my mother would chip my tail if she knew I made an agreement without proper tribute to the words. Sinking to my knees, my eyes drew level with Henri's mesmerizing topaz ones. Lifting her hand and placing it on my head between my horns, I stated the words of my homeland.

"An oath it is, Henri of Crossgate City. I will come to you tomorrow night or may the sun shatter my wings to dust."

"Oh," she breathed. "It wasn't that intense, dude. Um, thank you for agreeing to be my muse."

Releasing her hand, it slipped back to her side as I stood up once more. "My word is all I have left, and I offer it to you willingly." I began moving to the window when she stopped me a second time.

"Wait, you're leaving? Just like that?" she asked.

Placing one foot in the open window, I turned back to her, even as the call of the night air beckoned my wings. "I need to hunt, and you must gather your supplies. My obligations for tonight are already set, but I will seek you out when the sun sets again."

And I knew I must consult The Mistress about what I have done.

Henri nodded, taking a step back and tucking a curl behind her ear. "Damn, I have about a thousand more questions for you."

I chuckled, certain that she did. "I look forward to them," I mused.

Her lips pulled into a dazzling smile. "It's a deal then. See you tomorrow, Zendrax."

I met her smile with one of my own, rough as it must be and possibly the first that I'd had since my banishment. "Until tomorrow, Henri."

And I swept out the window, vanishing into the night's clouds.

# Chapter Four

## Henri

"I'm telling you! It was a huge freakin' gargoyle!" I took a long sip of my bubble tea and smacked my nearly empty cup down on the table, startling my two friends sitting opposite of me. "I know what I saw."

Chloe's hazel doe-eyes, just a shade lighter than her warm brown face, were bogged down with skepticism at my claims. Meanwhile, Simon refused to meet my glare as he nervously picked at the black chipping paint on his nails. Chloe sighed, seeing that she was going to have to speak for the both of them. Clearly, neither of my friends believed a word I'd said.

"I'm sure you saw something," Chloe said, turning back to me and reaching to put her hand over mine. "What if it was a maintenance guy?"

"He had wings, Clo, and it was almost midnight."

"You didn't go to a binger at Kent's, did you?" Simon finally chimed in, namedropping a guy we'd gone to university with. A guy who had a lot more in the money department than in the good grades department. Ended up dropping school and opening a brewery, and a damn good one at that. "I heard there was a big one last night. I also heard that the air was nice and clouded with various smoked goods."

"*No.*" As much fun as that sounded. "I wasn't at Kent's last night. I was in my apartment."

"You met this guy with no pants on?" Chloe asked, raising one eyebrow.

Couldn't argue with that. She knows me too well. "My panties were cute, at least," I grumbled.

"*Henri,*" Chloe groaned.

"The cat ones?" Simon asked, his face spreading into a toothy grin.

"I leave one pair to air dry on my dresser in the dorm and you're still hanging on to that four years later?"

Simon shrugged, smirking even as he avoided the question by taking a drink.

Pinching the bridge of my nose, I relented. "Fine, you two don't have to believe me, but I'm going to draw him. He's *gorgeous*, and it would be a waste not to. Speaking of which, I need to go to the Magical Muse to pick up supplies. Want to come with?"

"Ooh, fancy," Simon said, leaning over to look into Chloe's cup.

She scooted it away. "You have your own tea, Simon. And no thanks, Henri. I have a prior engagement."

"Are you working on a new furniture design?" I guessed.

"I'm modeling for a figure drawing class." She checked her phone. "I don't have enough time to go by Muse before I need to leave."

"I'll go. I've got nothing else going on," Simon said, then turned to Chloe. "Don't pick up any strays in class. We'll get jealous."

Chloe pursed her lips, trying not to smile. "Only you two dorks would make friends with your art class model. I think you're safe."

"What does that say about the one who befriended us back?" I teased, turning to Simon. "Thanks, I appreciate the company."

"Sure," Simon mused. "Even if you believe in gargoyles."

I pulled the straw out of my cup and flicked tea-drops at Simon. "Don't be an ass."

He laughed, grabbing a napkin from the dispenser to wipe the drops off his favorite black hoodie. "You know you love me."

"Oh, Henri, how is that sculpture coming? Any ideas yet?" Chloe asked.

"No," I groaned. "And I need to come up with something. Just a few months to finish a piece that big for a competition? I'm already pushing it."

"Whatever you do, make it flashy and minimize your flat edges," Simon added. "The mayor is one of the final judges, right? She came into the gallery and bought a ton of art for the new tourist board outbuilding going downtown in the city hall complex. She rejected everything my boss suggested that wasn't fluid with a lot of movement. Nothing modern, no buildings, no nothing."

"Urg!" I smacked my cheeks with both hands. "Buildings are my jam! Hard lines are my everything! How am I supposed to submit a tribute to an iconic symbol of Crossgate City when I can't use structures?"

"You'll think of something, I know it," Chloe soothed. "You're brilliant like that."

"Thanks, Clo." Discarding the straw and tipping my drink back, I chewed on the remaining tapioca balls from my cup and stood from the table. "I better go. I've got to get a few things and I should check the shop to see if any pieces sold."

Chloe and Simon stood too, tossing our empty cups on our way out the door. People crammed the street and sidewalks. The day was moderate compared to the swelter two weeks ago, hinting at the onset of autumn, and bringing out people to enjoy the day.

"I'll see you guys later," Chloe announced, turning the opposite way. "I parked my bike around back."

Waving her off, Simon and I took off down one of my favorite streets in Old Town. The buildings were tall and had character. The bright colors of the modern neon signs in the windows contrasted perfectly with the gray tones and red bricks of the antique structures. With every cobbled alleyway leading to the back of a shop, there were easily ten different details carved into corners and ledges that my fingers itched to replicate.

Simon fell into an easy conversation about his favorite band's new album while we walked. I fought the grin trying to overtake me as his hands joined in the conversation, adding an animated flair to a heated topic over which band member wrote the chorus to some song or other and why the lead singer would have done it better. It lasted all the way to the neon-orange front door of the art supply store.

"Hell yeah! A sale." Simon pushed open the door to Magical Muse, windows filled with highlighter yellow signs advertising a sale on paintbrushes. The bell over the door chimed a welcome, as did the instant warm rumbling on my leg.

"Hello there, Picasso." I lifted the fat orange cat, missing a front leg and sporting one handsome snaggletooth. He purred his welcome in my arms, butting his nose under my chin.

The woman who owned the art supply shop and attached consignment gallery was standing in the back corner, making sweeping strokes on a canvas with no rhyme or reason.

"Hey kids, call if you need me—but try not to need me! I'm feeling it today." Frizzy yellow hair and tie-dye yoga pants swayed to music older than my parents as Rita waved a brush in the air.

"Don't mind us, we'll just pay you in good vibes and get out of your way," Simon replied with sass as he disappeared to the back wall to inspect the display of discounted paintbrushes.

"Now that's a good trade!" Rita cackled.

Much to his dismay, I let Picasso down so I could peruse the aisle for the perfect canvas. It was easy to get lost in The Muse, and easier still to grow fond of the old hippie who ran it. Rita was a favorite among the students at Crossgate U, always willing to bitch about the professors like she knew them all personally. She would even bring in special order supplies for unusual assignments. And hell, maybe she knew all the professors. It was one of those stores that had the name imprinted in the very stone above the doors. Maybe it was here when the university was founded.

My fingers traced the edge of a stretched canvas, maybe four feet tall. It had a flaw in the canvas itself, and a big orange sticker marked it as a third off the original price. Could I afford it? I was already itching to capture Zendrax, and I knew a simple sketch wouldn't do. Whatever it took to convince the gargoyle to sit for me a few times so I could have a portrait, I'd do it. A flaw I could work with, I wasn't going to be selling this piece. But, speaking of selling pieces, I cleared my throat and turned towards the counter.

"Hey, Rita," I called, coming to the front with the large canvas in hand and a fluffy orange ball trying his best to trip me. "Sorry to hash your vibe."

"*Harsh* my vibe, chickadee," Rita corrected, slashing one last dramatic line of blue paint across her piece before dropping the brush in a mason jar and turning around with a wink. "That's okay. What can I do for you?"

"Can I check the gallery ledger for sales?" Shifting my weight back and forth to the beat of the music, I tried not to look too desperate, but the money would really help me out this month, and I wanted to buy this canvas more than I wanted to eat tomorrow. But, you know, I'd rather not go that route. Even with the discount, it was a large, expensive base for a personal project.

"Oh yeah, I think you did sell a couple things this week." Rita stepped through the curtain of the doorway behind the counter that connected the store to the gallery and brought back a leather-bound notebook. Licking her thumb and flipping through the pages, she smacked the middle of a page. "There we go, two prints of the bridge painting."

My heart sank. For all the original pieces I had in the gallery, especially the small stone carvings I'd poured myself into, the prints were the cheapest thing I had. I'd only done them on a whim, too, when Simon suggested it after the fancy-pants gallery he worked in started ordering prints to sell. And it wasn't that I didn't appreciate something I made had sold, but they would barely cover my next bubble tea let alone my electric bill.

"Thanks, Rita," I said. "I'll just roll it over, you don't have to pay me out so little—"

"And that sea serpent sculpture finally found his home!" Rita clapped the notebook shut, beaming at me.

A mix between a gasp and cough caught in my throat, ending badly as I grasped for a breath. "It did?"

One of my finals from my last year in school, I took inspiration from the large river that cut through the city not far from campus. I made the sea serpent from two pieces of stone, which looked like it was rising and falling in serpentine arcs out of whatever surface you placed them on. Hell, they could be bookends right now for all I cared. I was just glad to have the money, because I'd put a hefty price tag on it after Chloe's encouragement.

"Fuck yeah!" I whooped, startling Picasso at my ankle just as Simon came up with a fistful of brushes.

"It sold?" he asked. "I heard the last bit there."

"It went to the perfect home," Rita said, putting the ledger down and popping open the register. "A retired captain. Said he was pretty sure his boat had run into something just like it twenty years ago."

Simon laughed, laying out his brushes on the counter. "Now you're sounding like Henri. She thinks she's got gargoyles on her roof that move around."

I scowled at Simon as Picasso hopped up onto the counter, knocking half his brushes off in the process. "Ha! Serves you right."

"Oh, I think gargoyles could be real. Sea serpents, too." Rita nodded sagely as she divvied out the bills, sliding them and the ledger for me to sign off on my payment. "There's always stories going around of someone seeing something. Strange place, Crossgate City. That's why I like it here."

"You're both delusional," Simon scoffed, picking his brushes back up.

Rita shrugged. "Open your mind to it. Don't let your textbooks stop you from seeing things for yourself."

A very Rita answer, but one I was inclined to agree with as she forked over a pile of money that would keep me safely in my apartment for another month.

My apartment that was protected by an absolutely gorgeous gargoyle.

# Chapter Five

## Zendrax

The Crossroads vibrated as I landed behind it. A place of lights in impossible colors, music of intolerable volumes, and humans in uncomfortable numbers consuming alcohol. It was far more than I wanted to be around. So far, I'd contented myself with observing them from a distance, but to get to The Mistress I had to come to this place of wild abandon. Thankfully, within the confines of the 'club'—as she'd referred to it—lay a private staircase leading down to the alehouse for other creatures.

It was startling to find so many things roamed the streets of this realm that were little more than legend to me back home. Things that lurked in dark halls, things with fangs and wings and magic. Creatures that could appear human, yet would shed their skin in trade for fur or scale.

Stalking carefully around the corner, down to the private entrance where none of the humans would see me, I was able to relax, at least a fraction. Dangerous things lurked here, and while I easily considered myself one of them, I would still be wary of the patrons of this place. The Mistress was a being to contend with, certainly, but it still didn't ease my mistrust of the other creatures she allowed to lurk under her roof.

The dimly lit space featured black leather chaises with silks draped from a high ceiling, creating curtained alcoves along every wall. A long bar ran down one wall, the white marble flecked with gold, and a row of sleek stools were half-filled. Seductive music filled the space between the rumbling conversations of the hall, a fitting tone for a place filled with the musk of lust and sweat.

Heads turned my way as I took the first tentative steps into the strange space. A pink figure with long, pointed ears straddled something covered in dark fur as I passed the first alcove. Three feminine figures leaned over a fourth in the next partitioned booth. The one laying on the table was completely bare. A series of small cups of colorful alcohol sat in a line down her stomach as they each took turns indulging in whatever strange game they were playing.

It was the third recess that drew my attention and kept it. Some larger creature, closer to my build, with a brown, short-haired coat covering his body and large bull horns, sat on one of the chaises. He was naked for all I could tell in the dim lighting. His head fell back in pleasure as a demoness stroked her body up and down his stomach, his cock throbbing against her as she peppered him with taunting kisses. Henri's form filled my mind, though I didn't know why the demoness reminded me of her. What would the curious human who had first inspected my cock on the roof do in a similar situation? Would she be as playful as this demoness atop her partner? Would she be shy, or would she surprise me with something else entirely?

Shaking my head, I moved on with a frown. I was here for repentance, not to find a bedmate. I was just thinking about going back to my search for The Mistress when a cloven-hooved male brought me to a halt.

If Henri's undergarment was a collection of threads, this demon somehow wore even less. Toying with a chain that dangled from his golden collar, the demon offered me a drink from his tray.

"Welcome to The Crossroads," he purred with a wink and a flirtatious tone filled with invitation. "What can I offer you tonight?"

Glancing around, his dress was similar to several others in the room, or at least the gold collars and chains seemed to indicate the status of one who worked in this place. And if he worked for The Mistress, perhaps he could end my search now.

"I need to see your master," I answered.

Looking me up and down, he caught his bottom lip with a fang and held it while he decided on a response. "I don't have one at the moment, gorgeous, but I get off in about three hours."

My brow creased in confusion when a hand appeared on the male's shoulder.

A demon I recognized appeared, one that The Mistress called on by name when she first brought me to this place.

Stefan, I believe. Lean, tall, with curling horns that swept back from his face. His gray skin was almost tinted blue in a stark contrast to his white hair and horns. He looked troubled, holding a letter of some kind, then tucking it into his breast pocket. "Whoever is opening these portals under our noses is a pain in my ass," Stefan muttered. His eyes lifted and met mine, and he sighed.

Closing the last few steps, he placed a hand on the shoulder of the demon I had been speaking with. "I'll take it from here, see to room two. They're due some towels and refreshments."

The collared one bowed his head and left us, doing as he was bid. The demon that remained looked up at me curiously. "I don't think we've seen you since your first arrival. Let me see . . ."

He snapped his gloved fingers, and a notebook appeared from nowhere. I didn't let the magic startle me as it once had, but my teeth did press together a little tighter in my mouth.

"Zendrax, the gargoyle. You owe one boon to The Mistress. Currently living on the rooftops in Old Town. Ability to disguise among the humans: none. Housing needs: none. Susceptible to turning to stone during the day, particularly when ill or injured. Dietary needs: a wide variety but primarily spotted hunting for fish."

Stefan snapped his book closed, and it disappeared in a slight whisper of smoke. I bristled at the collection of notes.

"We have eyes everywhere." He shrugged, dismissing whatever concern he saw on my face. "What is it you've come for tonight? It doesn't look like you're here to indulge."

No, no. I was not. "I'm here to see The Mistress. I have a concern to bring to her about being seen by a human."

Stefan tightened his lips in a thin line, looking over his shoulder. "Follow me."

I did, and we left the large room of carnal silk alcoves. Golden figures, around two hands tall, lined the hallway. An array of creatures depicted splayed against the wall and held in place by shackles. Chains hung from their breasts or cocks, which carried heavy lanterns that gave off a sinful red light. What The Mistress built these rooms for, I could only guess, but my eyes lingered on one of the golden sculptures depicting a deliciously plump woman, her face contorted in a mix of pleasure and pain.

"Where were you seen?" Stefan asked, drawing me from my thoughts as we approached the door at the end of the hall.

"A rooftop."

Stefan's head snapped in my direction. A crease formed between his brows and his mouth hung open as if he was going to question me when the door flew open.

The door at the apex of the hall opened to reveal The Mistress herself. Alabaster hair slicked back, her choice of attire today, far more black and leather than what I now recognized as business attire from this realm than when she first appeared before me. A whip rested in a coil in her hand. Behind her, we could see two males cuffed to an odd bed. Covering the frame were loops and chains that held down the pair, panting and shining with sweat.

"What is it?" she asked, her tone not quite harsh, but we were both keenly aware we had disturbed her.

"He's been seen. Shall I contact the special agency?" Stefan asked.

Coal-red eyes slid to me, her face an unreadable mask. "What happened?"

I rolled my shoulders under the scrutiny of her gaze; it was like delivering bad news to a superior officer. "A human wandered onto the rooftop where I had been sunning for the day. She slipped and would have otherwise fallen from a deadly height."

The Mistress tilted her head, fingers playing with the handle of her whip. "No need. One human can be reasoned with. Bound to a deal, if need be. Take care of it, Stefan."

"Yes, Mistress." The demon beside me bowed, closing his notebook and allowing it to disappear once again.

"And you." Her tone was firm as she lifted the handle of her whip, tucking it beneath my chin as she managed to look down her nose at me, despite our height difference. "Do not forget the favor you owe me. I will be calling upon you soon."

I tensed as she took a step back into the space, closing the door as she turned her attention back to her partners. I'd not forgotten our bargain. Far from it, I had spent many nights pondering what deed she would coerce me into doing. But whatever she asked, I would obey. I owed her my life, and for the chance to repent in the name of my clan, I would see this bargain through.

Stefan sighed, running a hand through now disheveled hair as we walked back down the hall and to the main room once more. "It's always something. Ivor!"

A giant of a man behind the bar looked up, his blond hair shaved on one side and a large pegasus tattooed on his left arm.

"I have arrangements to deal with. Watch the club while I'm gone." Stefan barely waited for a nod before turning to me. "I need details on the location, the human's name, whatever you can offer me."

Defense clawed its way into my throat as I spoke. "What do you plan to do to her?"

Stefan snapped, a map of the city appearing in his hands. "I'm going to talk to her, obviously. She needs to be silenced."

"Silenced?" I said, louder than intended.

Stefan only glared at me. "I'm not going to kill her, if that's what you're thinking. You brutes are always ready to jump straight into violence. Whatever happened to striking a deal? A magical bargain?"

Eyeing the map, Stefan gestured to the part of town where I had found myself most at home among the tall structures. "Where exactly was this? You're not always on the same rooftop each day."

I was slow to respond, still unwilling to relent. That rooftop already felt like my domain, more so now that I had my first interaction in months atop it. I promised to keep the roof, and

Henri, safe. My wings were tense, my tail flicking back and forth at the tip in agitation.

"This one," I finally relented and placed a clawed fingertip on the map, pointing to the building I had spent more time on than any other in the city. He was right to ask, as I rarely chose the same roof two nights in a row, but that was about to change.

"I intend to keep in contact with her," I said. Hiding the fact now would go against my honor, and I would not hide my new interaction with Henri. I vowed to appear before her for the sake of her art, and I would not let this stop me.

"Yes, alright," Stefan said, his eyes not leaving the map. "Do as you will. Just don't bring any more headaches my way and keep out of sight of any more humans. Wait."

Stefan looked up, frowning at my legs. "Your nudity won't be a problem here, of course, but do you want something to wear in her presence?"

I hadn't considered it. Clothing wasn't unfamiliar to me, many of my kind wore it. I myself had done so most of the time, but what I was familiar with was unlike any design in this city, and the true rooftop statues I blended among wore nothing, so I had long ago discarded what I wore here. And yet, I had seen no nudity among the humans.

"Perhaps," I hesitated. "If you believe it to be the right course of action in this realm."

"It's much better if you do." Stefan waved a hand, a paper bag appearing as he handed it to me. "I think you're about the size of a minotaur, complete with tail. I think this will be the best garment for you. Try it on while I make a few notes on this human of yours."

From the bag, I pulled out a long, folded rectangle of cloth. A few straps told me it would fasten together somehow, but it took direction from one of the passing servers with her gold collar and chain and a look of appreciation as she directed my hands with the garment. Soon, I was wearing it around my waist, hanging down in some sort of war-skirt that didn't hinder my movement at all while still covering me. It was even gray—though not quite the color of my body—it would be close enough that it wouldn't stand out on the rooftop.

Stefan looked me over, tugging here and there until he adjusted it to his liking. Once satisfied, he rolled the map up and sent it away in a whisper of smoke before turning to face me. "Alright, Zendrax, I'm going to take care of it. Your human will be safe, as long as she cooperates. She must take a deal. For her safety, and the safety of the other creatures of this city. I will be gentle."

I nodded. "Good."

"Now, you go about your night, and I'll handle it. Farewell." Stefan disappeared. Much as he had sent away his notebooks and map, he left behind little more than a sigh of smoke as he vanished.

Curious eyes that had stayed on me since entering The Crossroads were now openly staring. Surely, they wanted to know what business I had with The Mistress and her closest hand. But I'd had enough of The Crossroads. The sights and smells only made me cross as I contended with the nature of this place; a comfort I would not partake in. Not in my period of repentance, not while I owed so much good to repay the failure of my people.

No matter how many times Henri had come to mind since setting foot in this den of worship for carnal desires.

I left swiftly, cooling my head in the night air as I swept into the dark clouds above.

# Chapter Six

## Henri

My hands were nothing but wrinkles when I set the last dish on the drying rack by the sink. With a satisfied sigh, I sank into a chair at the table, twisting the top on a well-deserved bottle of soda and enjoying the apartment's newly cleaned state. Small as it was, it was home. Over the years, I'd filled it with mismatched and thrifted furniture. A large table, still half-covered in supplies, albeit neatly stacked ones, took up the most room. A bed took up the slanted wall near the window outcropping, and an antique fireplace consumed the wall on the other side of that. Things got messy when I dove too deep into my art for days on end, but tonight I wanted to be at my best. When that sun went down, Zendrax was all mine.

Laughing, I had to set the drink down before I spilled it. All mine indeed, as if I'd know what to do with a seven-foot-tall creature of muscle and stone. But he'd agreed to let me draw him, and I wasn't going to pass up the chance for a good evening. All that was left was for the stupid sun to go down.

Gazing out at the view from my apartment, the neighboring buildings stood just as they always had, but now with so much potential. Were there other gargoyles? Could they be just over the next rooftop and I'd never know it? The lemon-scented cleaner I'd used entwined with fresh air from the large open window, drawing my eyes to the place where I'd thought about climbing out to again. I wanted to see Zendrax, but a healthy dose of acrophobia would probably keep me inside for the foreseeable future.

A knock at my door jolted me from my daydreams. It couldn't be Chloe. She'd be elbow-deep in sawdust in her workshop right now, making a stylish coffee table or something. Simon was on the other side of the river at a concert, so it wasn't him, as he wouldn't be missing a night out with his metalhead buddies to harass me.

So, who was it?

Padding across the apartment, I pulled the emergency sweatpants off the coat rack and yanked them on. Screw the fact that my home is a no-bra zone. Opening the door, I grunted, "Hello?"

The small hall at the top of the staircase was empty. I frowned, closing the door and turning around, only to scream.

A little taller than me, complete with bluish gray skin and curved horns, stood . . . something. Whatever it was, it was not human in the least. Though it did wear a nice dress shirt, all things considered. White hair neatly combed back, and a bored expression on its face completed an air of judgement and tedium.

"No need to scream, I assure you. You can call me Stefan. I'm here in regard to Zendrax, the gargoyle you saw last night." The creature, Stefan, gestured with a gloved hand to the window.

It was a good thing I put on pants. Grabbing the coat rack, letting a jacket fall to the floor in the process, I pointed the cheap aluminum rod at the intruder. "What about him?"

My heart was pounding in my ears. Was Zendrax okay? He wouldn't have told anyone about me, would he? I bit the inside of my cheek. Hadn't I done the same thing? I tried to convince Chloe and Simon of what I saw just this morning, so why would Zendrax have any such notion about keeping our encounter a secret when I hadn't done the same?

Stefan raised an eyebrow as he tipped the coat rack away from him with one finger. The other hand snapped, conjuring a notebook out of nowhere and sending a chill down my spine. This was real. This was really real, and Zendrax was clearly only the tip of the iceberg when it came to paranormal shit.

"Holy fuck," I hissed.

"Henrietta Prichard, second daughter of Harvy and Renee Prichard of Prichard Law. Older sister, Harriet Prichard-Marx, on track to take over the family business and is the clear family favorite."

"Ouch." I mean, it wasn't news to me, but to hear it from this stranger was extra uncomfortable.

"Attended Crossgate University, earning a degree in fine arts. *Somewhat* talented sculptor who dabbles in several other mediums."

"Hey! I'm very talented—"

"Small social circle, spends most of her time in her studio apartment and has aspirations to make a living off of her art to prove her family wrong." Stefan snapped the book shut, gesturing it away with a hint of smoke as he locked eyes on me. "Miss Prichard, I'll cut to the chase. I'm here to deal with the fact that you've witnessed a living, breathing gargoyle."

And a whatever-Stefan-is, but I wasn't about to add that out loud. I gripped the coat rack a little tighter, but I didn't point it at him again. Yet. "Are you here to kill me?"

Stefan's face turned disdainful. "Two of a kind, I see. No, Miss Prichard, I'm here to offer you a deal. You will never speak of what you see of the world the humans should not look upon, and in exchange, you will be allowed into the spaces The Mistress has approved for human guests of non-human associates."

Alright, so no killing involved. Probably. Setting the coat rack back down, I didn't let my eyes leave Stefan. He didn't make a move. If anything, he seemed tired.

"You just want me to stay quiet?"

Stefan hummed. "Well, it's more of a formality to induct you into the world of monsters. You'd be subject to our internal rules as well as our protections. Think of it as a . . . dual citizenship."

Monsters. A world of monsters. Monster was far from the first word that came to mind when I laid eyes on Zendrax, but I guess technically, it would be an accurate classification.

"What rules and protections?" I asked.

"Protections, as in a hands-off rule for you. From anything that preys on your species for sustenance, for example."

"And my friends Chloe Keita and Simon Laverda." The demand tumbled out of my mouth before I could even register what sort of creature would need humans for sustenance. Vampires? Probably vampires.

Stefan laughed. "You are indeed from a family of lawyers. Instant negotiation, I like it. Sure, I'll throw it in. Zendrax already owes The Mistress a boon, what's a little favor for his human. He did insist he be able to continue seeing you after all."

His human. I didn't hate the words. As loose as our association was, Zendrax was my first contact with a world I had no idea existed. And apparently, I meant something to him, too. Or maybe it was for his strange oath. He seemed the honorable type. Either way, I'd be seeing him again, and it filled me with excitement.

"What are the rules, then?" I asked.

Stefan was inspecting a piece of dirt on the fingertip of his white glove, already clearly done with this agreement. "The only real rule that will apply to you would be to not reveal the existence of anything inhuman."

"That's it? That's the only rule?"

He glanced at me, eyes going up and down in an invasive assessment. "Are you able to disembowel a fae? That's the last instance I remember witnessing of a breaking of the rules."

I blanched, taking a step back. "No."

"Then don't concern yourself with it." Stefan sighed, offering a hand to me. "Shake on the agreement and we can both go about our day."

This was wild. This was from a movie, or a novel, or something not from real life. And my parents would skin me for not getting a written contract, but what was the use of paper to bind an oath to a . . .

"What are you?" I couldn't help but ask.

"A contract demon in the employ of The Mistress."

Of course he was. That explained the horns. "If you're a demon, then are—"

"Please, Miss Prichard." Stefan's hand was still outstretched. "I am not here to unravel the mysteries of the universe to you. If you wish to learn more, have Zendrax bring you to The Crossroads. For now, I would like to be on my way."

Staring at the outstretched hand, I worked up my resolve enough to grasp it. His hand was huge, much larger than mine as he wrapped his long fingers around my grip and we shook. A chill ran through me, like a light switch flipping. Something in the nature of a change happening, though outwardly nothing had. All that had occurred was my agreement to this deal.

"Very good," Stefan said, and I didn't miss the way he wiped his hand on his pants. "Have a good evening, Miss Prichard."

He flickered out of existence. One minute he was there, and a heartbeat later there was nothing but a whisper of smoke drifting upward and fading away. I looked down at my palm, finding a crisp white card with "The Crossroads" in a glossy black logo and an address in tiny font. I flipped it over, and the back was blank.

"Weird," I whispered.

Standing in my apartment, staring at the space around me as if something entirely magical hadn't just happened, I let all the questions fly through my mind. If gargoyles and demons were real, what else was out there? Was this enough protection for Chloe and Simon? Where would I run into more of these creatures? Did I want to find more, or should I be blissfully ignorant? What was The Crossroads?

A flash in my window that happened every day about this time distracted me. A glare from the neighboring building as the sun went down for the night. I had only a little bit of time before sunset, and I didn't want him to see me in sweatpants and a university t-shirt with no bra.

Or did I?

No. No, I didn't. I think. I'd unpack that later. Right now, it was time to get ready to draw the most interesting specimen I'd ever get the chance to sit for me. Zendrax.

# Chapter Seven

## Henri

I scooted my table as far out of the way as I could get it. My sturdiest stool staged by the fireplace. On the stovetop, I was boiling the noodles for the most extravagant thing I could cook by myself, which is to say spaghetti noodles with sauce from a jar. Eyeing the fireplace, I wondered if I could get it lit in time. The nights were certainly turning cool, and while I didn't need it for the temperature quite yet, I did want to see what Zendrax looked like splashed in the flickering light.

A light tapping at the window made my eyes dart to the glass panes, hungry for another look at him. His wings were gloriously outstretched as he balanced on the outside of the window. That perilously small ledge not posing a problem for him at all. The window was still open, the tapping a formality for my sake, I'm sure. But I still rushed over to help him in. Not that he needed it, because all I really managed to do was hold the window at a slightly larger angle while he made his way in.

"You came," I breathed. "You're really real. I didn't make you up."

That brought a tight smile to his face. "Quite real, I assure you."

Then I noticed the kilt. No shirt or anything, and certainly no shoes over those clawed feet, but it was a change from last time. "You're wearing clothes now?"

A rude question, probably, but I didn't think that far ahead when I said it. Zendrax rolled one shoulder. "The statues are naked, and so I was naked to blend in," he said by way of explanation.

Good enough, I was just happy he was here. And I had to admire what that kilt was doing for him. His waist, still wider than mine but much more muscled, was wrapped up so tight. The kilt fell down and moved against his powerful legs in a way that accentuated them instead of hiding them. Coupled with the shirtless chest, it was doing something for me.

I swallowed. *Doing something for me? What am I, a perv now?* I tried to shrug off the odd thought. I was just attached to him, that's all. Nothing this interesting had happened to me probably ever, and now I had a friend, or something, from another world.

*Or something.*

My apartment suddenly felt so small. It had always been a studio, little more than a room with a bathroom attached to it if you excluded the curtained-off side where I did my messy carving work. The wall with the window where we stood now was where I'd chosen to put my bed, and I was keenly aware that if Zendrax backed up two steps, he could sit on it. But now that he was here, now that he had agreed for me to draw him, it was at least something safer to focus on.

"I'm all ready for you." I gestured at the stool next to the fireplace, regretting once again that I didn't think to light it before he arrived. The gargoyle eyed the stool before walking over to it and sitting down carefully. Testing the weight, maybe? From the creak in the floor, I suspected he weighed as much as he looked for a creature of living stone.

I smoothed my hands down my skirt. Nothing fancy, just a plain black dress that Chloe insisted was a staple I had to have in my closet. Something dark enough to hide charcoal smudges but would allow me to no-pants it while still being presentable if I ever needed to work on something with someone else there. I laughed at her at the store when she dropped it over the dressing room door, but I could kiss her for it right about now.

"I don't know if you're hungry, but I made dinner." I looked over at the pot of noodles that were surely done cooking by now. "It's not much, but you're welcome to have some. We may be here a while."

I reached for the pot and froze. The noodles were . . . a lot bigger now than when I'd first dropped them in the water.

"Shit," I hissed, turning off the burner and pulling the pot to the sink where the strainer awaited.

"Is everything okay?" Zendrax asked, already on alert for trouble.

"No! Yes, I mean. Stay there, I got it." Chewing my bottom lip, I strained the pasta and dumped it back into the pot. Picking up a piece, I bit into a slightly overdone but still very much edible noodle. At least that went okay.

As I added the sauce, I had to pull another jar from the cabinet to correct my measuring error, ending up with enough to feed a family of ten. Heavy footsteps behind me stopped a short distance away while I scrambled to find something big enough to serve the pasta in, eventually settling for a mixing bowl.

"Damnit." It came out as a whine, and I hated myself for it. I was no cook, and I shouldn't have tried. Not on a night that I was looking forward to. But one clawed hand reached to the edge of the bowl where a noodle was trying its best to escape. Plucking it free, I watched as Zendrax lifted it and ate it.

"I've wanted to try these," he said. Those jade eyes settled on my expression of wonder, and he smiled. Maybe the first earnest smile I'd seen from him so far.

I licked my lips, Zendrax tracking the motion carefully. "Oh," I managed.

"I see them being eaten on the streets below," he said. "Perhaps other kinds, as they are not usually in red sauce."

Noodles, he was talking about noodles.

"You probably see people eating ramen from the place around the corner," I said. "They taste very different from this, but they're all called noodles."

He nodded, his face now one of concentration as he sighed. "This world holds so many things I do not know."

I didn't know how to respond. He was obviously conflicted about something. He said he was from another realm, but not why he left or how he came to be here. Originally, I had thought I could ask about some of that tonight, but in the moment, with his sad and frustrated expression, I couldn't.

"Let me get the plates out and you can eat all you want." There was certainly enough to go around.

I brought plates and silverware down and a cheap bottle of wine. Extra sweet, the only way I'd drink it. Zendrax took the initiative and brought over the spaghetti. I couldn't complain, it was a heavy bowl.

He watched my movements with a careful eye. I moved slowly, showing off everything I did from twirling the noodles onto my fork to taking a bite. He mimicked my motions, the fork comically small in his hands.

*Note to self: get one of those giant serving forks if I ever have a gargoyle over for dinner again.*

When I poured him a glass of wine, his mouth played into a smirk.

"An entire realm away, and yet humans still ferment fruits." He closed his eyes as he smelled the glass, then drank.

"I'm glad you found something familiar here. Any foods you miss? What do you usually eat?"

Zendrax set his glass down, looking over his shoulder towards the window. "Fish, mostly. As for what I miss, there was a grain that would be pounded to a mash and cooked into hard sticks. Salty, earthy. Sometimes with vegetables cooked into it. I haven't seen anything like it here, but I'm eager to try the foods of this realm."

His eyes drifted back from the window and landed on me with warmth. "Thank you for sharing a meal with me. It has been a while."

Lonely. Loneliness overflowed from his words, and my chest tightened at the thought. When I left home, proclaiming my life as an artist against my parents' wishes, I thought I was lonely. But I quickly met Simon, then Chloe, and Rita and Picasso and so many other people who were a part of my life now. But Zendrax, he didn't appear to have anyone. Except maybe the demon from earlier.

"I met Stefan today."

He froze. I didn't expect such a reaction out of the stoic gargoyle, but his face flooded with caution. "What happened?"

He wasn't upset, per se, but he was paying close attention. So, he did know Stefan.

"He showed up here and made a deal with me. I already know about you, and now him, so I agreed to keep the world of monsters a secret. His words," I corrected, "not mine. I don't think you're a monster."

That allowed him to relax, at least. He shifted, that beautifully sculpted jaw edging toward the window as he gestured. "There are monsters out there, Henri. Don't be fooled by appearances. And I hold no scorn for the word, because when it comes to monsters, I promise you I am one of them."

That sent a shiver through me, but I didn't hate it. He was right, I'm sure. Those claws, the horns, the wings, the tail. Not only did he have the otherworldly appearance that would bring the word "monster" to mind, he appeared to have the muscles to back it up. A warrior, he had called himself. I believed him.

The rest of the meal consisted of me finishing my spaghetti and watching in awe as Zendrax downed the first plate in minutes. Then a second, then a third, before I offered to pack him up the rest for later. It was a good thing I'd inadvertently made so much. He clearly needed a home cooked meal more than I did, and my heart sank when I saw it on his face. He'd been so alone that even food had lost its warmth for him. I couldn't picture it. Being responsible for my every meal with no chance of takeout or a grocery store. No one to eat with, no friends talking over bubble tea or laughing at the joke of the day from the old man who made my shrimp fried rice. Nothing.

But he didn't need me to point that out. He was the one living that life. But if I could help it, he wouldn't be so alone anymore. He'd have a friend, if he wanted one.

"Thank you for the meal." His tone was soft and content and so, so happy over a plate of overcooked noodles and convenience store sauce in a jar.

"It was nice to eat with someone," I said, the truth shining through for me as well as him. "I'd love to have you over for dinner again sometime. It's nice to have a friend."

# Chapter Eight

## Zendrax

Friend. Was I worthy of such a thing? Exile spared me my life, but with the pretense that I would repent my failure and live a life of worthy deeds. Where did forging new relationships fit into that? But Henri glowed, a star that demanded you look upon its light when the rest of the sky was dark and grim. Not only had she offered friendship, but she had already brought the first smile to my face in many months. She offered me food, cooked by her own hands. She found something appealing in my presence, a desire to create art after looking upon the defeated stone of a banished gargoyle.

My chest tightened. Of course, she wasn't aware of my banishment. That I was a disgrace to my clan and kind. And yet, despite knowing I did not deserve her kindness, her shining light, I could not turn away from the torment of her smile. A reminder of every reason I should not covet her company. But after months of solitude, I was too weak willed to resist her. And, perhaps, if there was anything I could do for her, I could begin my repentance. My period of mourning was over, but I yet struggled to find ways to help in this foreign realm.

"It would be an honor to be your friend, Henri," I murmured. The timbre of my voice had never allowed for secrecy and whispers, and I knew she heard me when her lips parted in surprise. A sunset blush raced across her cheeks, glowing between the dots of brown stars that covered her skin.

"It's not that intense." Her laugh was strained, affected. Curious that such a light would have any reason to doubt that her attentions were anything less than a treasure. I'd met many humans in my time, and the brave, talented, curious Henri was a rarity. What, or who, would cause her to act in such a way when treated as a blessing?

"Let me clean up and we can get started," Henri said, rising from her seat. A diversion from her embarrassment, but I was in no position to ask about it. We each had our secrets, it would seem.

Once she cleared the table and put the rest of the food away, she directed me back to the stool by the fireplace. Large and sturdy, I judged it would hold a gargoyle and sat down.

"However you want to pose, just do so comfortably," she said. "This part takes me a while."

With a nod, I leaned back against the side of the fireplace and crossed my arms over my chest. I could rest this way for hours while watching over a wall or tower or battlement. And if she needed me to do so, I would remain here all night.

"Perfect." She scooted her chair to the large canvas she had at the ready, another chair next to it, holding her supplies and a bottle of water.

"Do you like music? I usually put on jazz or something soft," she said.

Music. I'd heard music at The Crossroads, and I dreaded more of its like. But Henri was my only friend, and if she wanted to enjoy her music while she worked, she would have it. I nodded. "Anything you like."

"Right, we probably don't have music like you had back home." She picked up her phone—I'd come to learn it did a great many things if you knew which buttons to press—and from the table by her bed a calamity of string instruments erupted.

"Sorry!" She fiddled with the phone again and the volume decreased until it was a tolerable level. "There, I hope you like orchestra music. I can't listen to stuff with lyrics when I'm working for some reason."

It was absolutely nothing like the sounds that came from The Crossroads. It was soft and swift and alive, and I offered her a genuine smile. "I like it."

She beamed at me, and with that, she began to work. It was a curious thing, to watch an artist at her craft. She'd already shown me some of her drawings, but to witness her in action was different. Though she was normally quick to smile, her face now hardened in concentration as her hands moved in swift, bold strokes. Her eyes darting between the canvas and where I sat. It was a strange feeling, to be the subject of an artist. But if it offered me time with Henri, if it would make her happy to do so, I would gladly sit for her art.

I studied her as she studied me. She didn't even notice that my gaze traced her shape in that black dress. Such a color was reserved for royalty in my realm, but I'm so glad it wasn't in this one. It suited her, wrapping her shape in the dark of a night's sky while the rest of her mesmerized me entirely. The shine of her hair, the fascination of the markings on her skin, the roundness of her hips and full thighs. The varied shapes of humans had always fascinated me, and I decided that the shape of Henri was possibly my favorite.

After a while, she put down her charcoal and opened her bottle of water. "We don't have to be silent if you don't want to. I've got a ton of questions for you, if you don't mind me asking. You don't have to answer anything uncomfortable. And if you have questions for me, I'd be happy to do the same."

There was that curiosity again. "Anything you want to know, Henri."

It was the right answer, apparently, because the questions exploded out of her with a beaming smile. "Are there more of you? Where did you come from? How did you get here? Can you feel things with your skin?"

Seeing as how she had abandoned her work for the moment, I adjusted how I sat on the stool, leaning forward with interest. Henri was abuzz with questions, the fiery curls bouncing around her shoulders as she moved.

"There are more of my kind where I come from, but I haven't encountered any in this realm. I am of the Stoneforge clan, guardians of Stoneforge Castle. Or we were. Until a battle devastated our numbers."

Her posture softened. "Oh, I'm sorry."

"You were not a part of it, Henri. There is nothing to apologize for." I shook my head. "It was many months ago now. I lost most of my clan, and I . . ." *I was banished.* The words were difficult to say out loud to someone I wanted to maintain this new and fragile friendship with. What would she think of me if she knew?

"We don't have to talk about it," she said. "I have things that are hard to talk about, too. Can I ask other questions? Nothing about your home, I promise."

Considerate. So considerate, this little artist. I reviewed the questions she had already asked and moved on to the next one. "I can feel things on my skin, just as you can. I do not know if it is more, or less sensitive than yours, but I have sensation on every surface of my body."

Her eyes flicked down to the garment I now wore, then to my wings, then to my tail. She was burning with curiosity, and I chuckled. "You may touch me, if it would please you."

She moved from her seat in an instant, already on her feet and walking toward me with her eyes fixed on my chest. As she drew closer, I could still smell the wine from her breath and the floral hints from her soap. Henri's dark topaz eyes shone brightly as she reached out her calloused artist's hands, fingertips brushing against the round of my shoulder as though it entranced her. Her palm was warm as she slid it flush to my shoulder.

"You're cold," she said, her attention moving to my face but her hand remaining where she placed it. "Do you need a blanket? Or I could light the fireplace."

"No, it doesn't bother me. The temperature of a gargoyle will remain roughly the same as the surrounding environment. The night turns cool, and so do I."

Her pink tongue darted out to lick her lips, even as she noted the cool, dark night outside the window. "That's fascinating. And you don't mind it?"

"Do you mind the feel of the air on your skin? It's no different to me."

"Interesting." Henri moved her hand from my shoulder, tracing fingertips along my collarbone. I didn't miss that her eyes lingered, moving down my chest and stomach. Was the garment I wore a mistake? The thought left me quickly as her hands found a new target in the form of my wings.

Her fingertip traced the thin membrane between the harder structural frame, a part of any winged creature that is sensitive enough to feel the air currents. And I was no exception. A hiss escaped me, my tail reaching around to curl around her ankle as I grabbed the wrist of her outstretched hand.

Startled, she froze in place, then moved to see what wrapped around her ankle. I unwound the end of my tail, shifting it out of the way again and letting go of her wrist. "I apologize. My wings have more sensation than most of my body."

"Oh." Henri snatched her hand to her chest. "I didn't mean . . . sorry."

There it was again. That unwarranted apology. "You didn't know, and it only caught me by surprise. By all means, try again if you're curious."

Her touch would drive me mad, but I would endure it. It had been a long time since I had this kind of gentle interaction. Longer still since I last allowed an intimate touch against a part of me that felt so intensely. But she didn't need to know that. All she wanted was exploration.

Henri's hand reached out, and her featherlight touch ran along the outer rim of my wing, nearly pulling a groan from me. So soft. Too soft, but I held my position. Her hands continued their advances in agonizing lines down my wings before moving to my horns.

"Here?" Henri asked, gently touching one finger to the base of a curved horn.

"Not very sensitive," I answered, grateful that I sated her curiosity before I could voice what she'd truly done to me. Her scent was now entwined with mine, her touch along my arms, chest, wings leaving her essence in the wake of her fingertips. But to inspect my horns, she had to reach up higher than her stature would allow. I could bend over, craning my neck to allow her access, or . . .

"Woah!" Henri squealed as I placed my hands on either side of her waist, lifting her until she could sit on my knee for better access to my horns.

"You sure aren't one to mind personal space, are you?" Her words were scolding, but her tone wasn't, and she settled her arms around my shoulders as she found her balance.

"I did not want you straining yourself to reach."

Our faces were so close now. I hadn't intended for this closeness, but I couldn't say I felt disappointed with the opportunity to study Henri as well. Her eyes were so filled with wonder and questions as they traced the lines of my face that I felt the urge to do the same.

"May I touch the stars of your face?"

Her brows drew together. "My what?"

"The decorations of your skin, the many stars scattered like the night sky across your face," I tried to explain.

That brought a bubbling laugh to Henri, a charming sound that warmed me. "They're called freckles. Are there no humans where you come from?"

"There are, but they do not have stars on their skin. May I touch yours? Do they hurt?"

She took my hand with her tiny one, guiding it to cup her cheek. "They don't hurt. See? They're flat against the rest of my skin. It's a genetic . . . actually, I don't know what it is. Some kind of genetic mutation we got along the way? I have them all over the place, not just my face."

She gestured to her arms. But my mind was more curious about how they traveled down the rest of her body. What lie beneath the dress that clung to her shape? I paused. It was a dangerous line of thought. While not common, it wasn't unheard of for a human to take a gargoyle to bed in Stoneforge. But that honor was reserved for a gargoyle who was not banished, disgraced.

I shook my head, startling Henri again, and averted my eyes. Her scent, her closeness, her beauty. It was disturbing my banishment, my mission, my failure. And yet, I couldn't resist it.

"Is everything okay?"

"I have done you a disservice." I stood in one motion, holding Henri until I could set her safely on her feet. "I will go. If you need me again, I can return another night."

"What's wrong? Did I do something?" Her expression turned to distress, panic. "I'm sorry."

"*No*," I said. "You have done nothing wrong, Henri. You are a bright light in my night, and you have done nothing wrong. Do not apologize when you are not at fault."

Her shoulders sank. "Then can I still draw you another night? Or make dinner? If it was the spaghetti, I can order takeout next time."

I placed a hand on each of her small shoulders, my fingertips sinking into her softness and warmth. "Henri, I must go for my own conscious. You have done nothing wrong. I will return in a few days if you wish."

"Yes." She placed a hand over mine on her shoulder. "Please."

The conflict on her face, the conflict within me, struggled to let go. We both parted, and I swept towards the window. "You are a kindness I did not expect to have, Henri. I will be good to you, and all will be safe under my rooftop. Be well."

Pulling open the window, I barely touched a foot onto the sill before gliding out into the night.

# Chapter Nine

## Henri

Nothing helps shake off a bad night like waking up to a walk in the park with a hot coffee in my hands and the rustling of autumn winds in the trees. And boy, did last night count as a bad night. I didn't know where I went wrong with Zendrax, but I wanted desperately to fix it. Of course, for that to happen, he would either have to show back up or I would have to get over my newfound problem with the dizzying height of the roof. My stomach turned the moment I pictured the drop, my body starting to tremble and tense, as if remembering the near-death experience Zendrax had saved me from. The flashbacks of that moment had been the inspiration for more than one nightmare since it happened.

*Nope, not going to think about that right now.*

The cinnamon hazelnut drink warmed me from my lips all the way down my throat as I walked the meandering path in Riverview Park. Just a normal, pleasant walk in the park that had nothing to do with the gargoyle that made my heart ache or my newfound fear of heights.

Tucking my hair mostly into a soft white hat and wriggling into my control top leggings, I was welcoming the incoming fall weather with a reverence only a fat girl who was tired of boob sweat and chub rub could. The park wasn't huge, but it was in a very busy part of the city, south of the river, where a good chunk of the business district stood. The nearby shops and towering buildings were nostalgic, reminding me that my high school was just blocks away and the pizza place that had been my first job was close as well. And this coffee.

Taking another sip, I made my way down the last few steps of the branch of sidewalk I had chosen. Stepping between two large magnolia trees, I looked out at the fountain in need of a statue. The pinnacle of this whole contest, and why I was wracking my brain for ideas. The fountain wasn't much in the way of water, basically a square platform with a moat and a few bubbling jets that could light up at night. However, that platform was the throne upon which the winner would have their work displayed, complete with a brass commemorative plate that just needed an artist's name and the title of the sculpture. A few more steps and I could brush my fingers across the newly placed sign. What I wouldn't give for my name to be on it, and my art to be on that platform. Something about it felt so real, so tangible. Sure, I'd stayed afloat selling my art so far, a few commissions had landed me my beloved flat in the first place. Winning a city-wide competition to have my art displayed for the public? If that couldn't convince me my family was wrong and I could be a true artist, I didn't know what else could.

Taking a long sip from my cup, I took a seat at a nearby bench where I could stare at the fountain. Whatever went there could only be so big at the base, but there was room for movement and form in the empty air above. Simon had told me to steer away from hard edges, but what did that mean, really? The mayor didn't have an eye for the designs I preferred, but luckily, there were other judges involved.

*Maybe I should go with my gut and make something that would be a masterpiece to me and not create for someone else's eye.* Though that was the smarter way to go about it when you wanted to sell art. Did I hope to luck out and win the committee over with my style, or should I go for a shape that I knew would please at least one of them? Hmm.

I sat on the bench until my coffee was nearly gone, staring. Thinking. Waiting. Just passing the time and willing inspiration to strike me. The day was lovely and people filled the sidewalks, either on leisurely walks or office workers getting in hurried steps on their breaks.

"Dammit." I stood, chucking my empty cup into the nearby bin and stretched my arms out in front of me, stiff from sitting in the cool air, no more inspired than when I'd sat down.

"Henrietta?"

Freezing, I let that voice sink in. We hadn't spoken in months, and even then, it was a barely passing hello at a family friend's funeral. Turning around, I met a face so similar to mine. Pale, with a million freckles and high cheekbones. Her nose a bit longer, thinner. Her chin daintier. But her face was unmistakably related to mine.

"Hey, Harriet," I greeted my older sister.

The first thing she did, the first thing she always did since we'd moved out of our parents' house, was to eye me head to toe. Gritting my teeth, I shielded my face into something neutral in preparation for whatever she was about to say. There was no mistaking the name-brand suit she wore or the lapel pin with the family law firm's logo on it. Her hair, which by all accounts should be just as hard to manage as mine, swept back into an elegant French braid. Not one orange coil out of place.

"You look . . . well," she offered curtly.

It was a non-answer. A compliment without any meat to it, which was certainly Harriet's style. Polite fluff with no substance, even to her own sister. One of us had really taken to the country club life under Mom's tutelage, mastering the art of pleasant nothingness, and it wasn't me.

"You look like Mom's younger twin," I offered back, at least presenting her with some truth. She could take it as a compliment if she wanted to, but I wasn't going to reach any further for her than she did for me.

She did little more than raise an eyebrow, then scanned the area where I'd been sitting. "What brings you out here?"

I balked. "Are you asking out of politeness or real interest?"

She pursed her lips. "I can take an interest in my own sister, Henrietta."

"You can't even take enough of an interest to say my name right, *Harri*," I spat. "You know what? I don't have time to deal with this. I don't want your small talk, and I don't want you to eye my clothes like one of your precious country club friends, and I certainly don't want you to keep staring down your nose at me as if we didn't share a childhood. I came out here for inspiration and peace, neither of which you can give me."

Turning on my heel, I walked off in the direction from which I'd arrived.

"You're such a child, Henrie—*Henri*," she called. "I honestly came to see how you were doing. I can see this park from my office, you know."

Cursing at myself, I remembered she was right. I could look over my shoulder right now and see the floors of a nearby building that my family occupied with their law firm, illuminated by the big white letters on the second floor that spelled out my last name. Gritting my teeth, I turned to face her again. "I appreciate the thought, but if it takes me being right under your nose to have your attention, I don't want it. The last thing you said to me was that I'd end up back at the firm answering phones within a year. Well, it hasn't happened yet, has it?"

Harriet threw her hands up and let them fold across her chest. "I'm sorry, okay? I'm allowed to worry for my baby sister. I don't want to see you waste your life struggling. I never said you should give up your art. Keep it as a hobby if that makes you happy. Dad still goes golfing most Sundays. You could do something like that, I'm sure."

"And when was the last time you played your violin?" I asked. "Exactly what time do *you* get to spend on hobbies while working at the firm? Dad is semi-retired. You're probably working your ass off to earn your place as partner before the others start screaming 'nepo baby' at you."

She frowned. "I've lost interest in the violin."

"You could have been a professional. Your orchestra teacher said it all the time. Your private tutor is on the Crossgate City Symphony. You had every opportunity to run with it and you didn't," I countered.

"I would never have been happy with that life," she scoffed.

"And I would never be happy in that office! Are you not seeing the hypocrisy here? We're two different people, and just because you and Mom and Dad can't see an artistic lifestyle for yourselves, that doesn't mean you get to keep shitting on *me* for choosing it."

Her perfectly organized face scrunched up. "I just don't understand why you insist on struggling when Mom and Dad laid out the groundwork for us to have *incredibly* respectful careers. People would kill for this kind of opportunity."

"For fuck's sake, Harriet." I sighed through my nose. "You're not getting it at all."

Mom, Dad, and in recent years, Harriet all had the ability to make me feel small and less and beneath them. But I'd suffocate in that office with the desks and paperwork and water cooler chitchat. The daily grind and the tiptoeing legal jargon. At least with my art, I could breathe. It was so much more than a career for me; it was a creative urge inside that I had to let out somewhere, somehow, or else I'd explode.

"Art is a respectable career. That's the problem," I huffed. "You sound just like Mom. You don't respect what I do, but my art has allowed me to live on my own this whole time. Years, Harriet. I just wish you could see it the way I do."

"Henri . . ." she tried, but I was already walking away. Harriet didn't need to see the tears forming or the wobble of my lip. Maybe in a few more years we'd both grow up enough to reconcile, but while she was still so captivated with every word that left Mom's lips, there would be this wall between us. I just hoped we didn't stubborn ourselves right out of being sisters until we were old and gray or one of us died.

But even if that's what was in store for me, I'd live with it long before I gave up who I am to please everyone else.

# Chapter Ten

## Henri

Nothing like throwing yourself into your work to forget about your asshole family. At least, I'd been trying to do just that as I'd sharpened and polished my tools, picked at my smaller scraps of stone to whittle into nothing-shapes and idle my time away. I was a mess, my place was once again a mess, and the small carvings I'd managed to make were mediocre at best. I eyed the simple bear on my table and sighed as I scooted away from it. Maybe I could still put it in the gallery at Magical Muse.

At least it was a distraction. But my family wasn't the only thing I needed distracting from. The large, elegant form of a certain gargoyle wouldn't leave my head for more than an hour at a time. The half-sketched canvas staring at me from the easel wasn't helping either, that's for sure. It had been days since he'd left. The only logical conclusion was that I made Zendrax uncomfortable. My gut twisted every time I thought about the pain on his face as he left the apartment. How it had been my fault, my touch, my interest that drove him off. But I couldn't help myself. I felt drawn to him, fascinated by him. A really attractive gargoyle, who spoke like a gentleman, with arms as big as trees, *and* he respected my art. Who wouldn't like that? Nothing fun or interesting ever happens to me, and here I was meeting a living, breathing gargoyle. And . . . touching his sensitive wings.

"What the hell is wrong with you, Henri?" I moaned before shoving my dust-covered work clothes in the hamper and pulling on an old t-shirt. Not that'd I'd gotten any actual work done for the last two days. Mindlessly, I'd carved away at the empty spaces of what would be a sculpture of something or other; I hadn't decided yet. But after Zendrax left me the other night, I hadn't had the will to concentrate in earnest, knowing it was my fault he felt distressed. That had to be it, right? I was pushing the limits. He'd told me it was fine, but was it really? Now that I knew it bothered him, I felt like trash. Shoving the toothbrush in my mouth to wrap up my bedtime routine, I stared at myself in the mirror.

Okay, time to review the facts. My first thoughts of Zendrax were how gorgeous he was, followed by an immediate interest in his cock. Because I'm a sleazy bastard like that. I didn't know he wasn't a statue at the time, but the fact remains, I still felt the guy up. And then he saved my life in an epic once-in-a-lifetime move. And his manners? Almost an over-the-top respect for others. Attracted to him? I was ready to be putty in his hands. His incredibly inhuman hands.

I spit in the sink, washing off my toothbrush. The desire to screw something of a different species. What kind of sexual deviancy was that? And here he was, being more than a gentleman. Clearly, he needed social interaction and a hot meal, not whatever filth was going through my mind.

Bathroom routine finished, I padded over to my bed and fell into it. At least I had gotten a good start to the drawing, and I knew now that I wanted it in oils by the time we were done. I had to paint Zendrax; I hadn't wanted to paint something so bad in a long time.

I groped blindly at my nightstand, looking for a scrunchie, when my hand fell on a small piece of paper. Lifting my head, I looked over to see the business card from Stefan. Sitting up, I snatched the card off the table and looked at it. A sleek logo in glossy print promising a sexy club from the look of it, and an address. I knew where that was, or so I thought. Near the river, at least.

Stefan said I could learn more about the world of monsters there. It was thrilling and scary at the same time, but did I want to go? It could be a chance to find out more about Zendrax's world, or at least what he wanted to protect me from. And Stefan said I'd be safe. But it could be a trap, an easy way to lure human girls to the monsters. Then again, Zendrax seemed to know Stefan and showed little concern about his visit. And I trusted my gargoyle, even with all the sadness of the world in his eyes.

"Okay, we're doing this." I hopped out of bed and ran to the closet. The little black dress wasn't the only thing I had courtesy of the shopping sprees with Chloe. One set of black booty shorts and a see-through pink crop top with my favorite black bra, perfect for a club. Was it too much? I guess I'd find out when I got there, but this fat girl can dance, and I was ready to do so if it meant learning more about these monsters.

It was easy enough to get a car from Old Town to the river. I took my coat because it was cold and I wasn't about to walk down the street in what I was wearing underneath, but it felt exhilarating to be out for the night. Chloe and Simon got a quick text that I'd be on Bridge Street, and I had my self-defense keychain kit, just in case. Not that it would do much if the monsters were all like Zendrax or had magic like Stefan, but it couldn't hurt.

My strappy-heeled foot hit the sidewalk, placing me in the neon glow of Bridge Street. As underdressed for the night air as I was, I wasn't out of place in this part of town that was clearly built for the nightlife. Oddly enough, it wasn't until I took my first steps forward and closed the car door that my nerves hit my stomach. This was a bad idea, a *really* bad idea. And I realized it all too late as I stood on the side of the busy street and watched my ride drive away.

*Deep breaths, you can do this. Just go to the club, have a drink at the bar, and observe. You're good at observing. That's why you're an artist.*

Pulling the card from my purse one last time, I double-checked the address and walked to join the line to get into the club. The line wasn't terribly long, but it would still be a wait in the cold. The excited groups waiting in line kept mostly to themselves. It seemed like a popular place, but I hadn't heard of it when I was in college, and I wasn't sure why unless it was new. Once I got closer and took another look at the sign above the door, I groaned.

"Shit." The logo was similar, but not the same. I pulled out the card from Stefan and looked again. I had the address right, so where was The Crossroads?

"Is everything alright?" The bouncer at the door must have overheard me. He cocked his head to the side. His hair, shaved on one side, allowed a dramatic waterfall of blond to fall on the other.

I had to look over my shoulder to make sure it was me he was talking to and not someone else. "Me? Yeah, I think I got in line at the wrong club."

A smattering of laughter surrounded me, and my cheeks heated. Even the big guy at the door was laughing until he saw the card in my hand.

"Where did you get that?" He pointed to my hand, and I frowned, holding up the card.

"This? From an . . . acquaintance?" He raised an eyebrow at me. "Named Stefan?"

"Stefan gave you that?" The blond giant at the door moved from the front of the line. He walked over to where I stood, bringing all the eyes in the line to our interaction. I held up the card for him to see and a slow smile spread across his lips.

"You're not far off. I'll show you the way." He lifted the rope, and I ducked under to follow him, protests and grumbling followed behind me all the way to the front of the line.

Just as we neared the door, another bouncer-looking dude in a dress shirt with a buzz cut nodded to the blond giant next to me. "Thanks for watching the door, Ivor. I'm back now."

"Anytime, good luck with the line." The giant, Ivor, turned away from the line and began walking along the outside of the building and away.

"Wait, where are we going?" I asked, my hand drifting to the stabbiest tool on my self-defense keychain.

"Around back. You're going to The Crossroads, right?" He looked over his shoulder at me as he passed into the alley at the side of the building, his gaze drifting down to what I was holding as he chuckled. "That won't do you a lot of good in here, but if you're under Stefan's protection, no one here will touch you."

"Good," I swallowed. "Good to know."

He took us to a nondescript door next to a dumpster. If this was some kind of speakeasy situation, and they did a damn good job of making it look uninteresting. Running away crossed my mind. So did screaming if the door opened to a black pit of nothingness. But when Ivor opened the door and a soft red glow illuminated a perfectly normal staircase, complete with thrumming music coming up from downstairs, I relaxed.

"Welcome to The Crossroads." Ivor winked as he held the door open for me. I offered a strained smile and proceeded down the stairs. The atmosphere started to feel more and more comfortable as I saw barstools at the bottom and the matching logo painted along the wall that went down. This was the right place, at least.

"Have a good time, human," Ivor called behind me just before letting the heavy door drop shut.

I stopped, turning around to stare up at the exit, but I was all alone. The music below had a sexy beat, and a cackling laugh made me jump and look where I was going. This was a club, alright. The smell of sweat and the roar of sounds were plentiful. Down I went into the club below.

A coat closet at the bottom of the stairs was my last defense between me and the open club. A debate waged a silent war within me as I wondered if I had chosen the right clothes for this. How much attention did I want to draw to myself? Or would the big coat be more conspicuous?

"Screw it." I hung my coat on a hook and stepped into the club with my chin up and shoulders back.

To call this place sexy would be an understatement. Fabric draped from the ceiling made little spaces of privacy where bodies moved. It was so dark in here that I had a hard time telling what was going on in the little niches, but I had a feeling I was better off minding my own business. Another wall of the space had less draped silk but more bodies, and the thrum of the music elicited dancing and grinding.

The bar, however, was well lit and gorgeous. A masterpiece of marble in one continuous slab. White with gold flecks in it, the lightest of gray streaks flowing like rivers across the surface. How the hell did they keep it from chipping and scratching as a bar?

*Well, I know how to find out.*

The moment I moved into the open space, crossing to an empty barstool, I felt eyes on me. I decided to go with tunnel vision and focus on the empty seat as my goal and nothing else. I could look around later when I had a drink in me. Or three.

Sliding onto the seat, I locked eyes with the bartender, a woman with pink skin and . . . horns. It wasn't quite as shocking as when I screamed my head off at Zendrax on the roof, but it was still a lot. I knew I was staring, but she was very professional as she popped the top off a glass bottle for another patron before coming my way.

"Hey, sugar. First time at The Crossroads?" She propped an elbow on the counter, her other hand playing with a long gold chain dangling from a matching collar around her slender neck.

"Hi, uh, yes. Is it that obvious?" I winced.

She waved. "Don't worry about it. So, who are you fucking to get a pass to show up here?" She smirked. "Or maybe I should ask, what you're fucking?"

My face heated even as the smile spread across my face. "Is that really the only reason a human would be invited here?"

She shrugged. "It's the usual answer. I'm Tanya, by the way. Can I get you a drink?"

Okay, I could do this. A part of me was terrified of Tanya, but she was smaller than me and friendly. I'd already seen Stefan, and I'd been up close and personal with Zendrax, so this should be easy.

Right?

"Yeah, can I get a mojito?"

"You got it." Tanya winked as she dropped the gold chain from her hand and turned to the shelves. With the opportunity to look around from a more comfortable place, I sought out the safest places to stare.

Down the bar from me, there were a number of people. They looked human, mostly, except one that had wings and another that was a bull. A furry come to life or something. No, wait, those had a name. Minotaur? A minotaur. I think. But when a bulky guy with about a hundred piercings leaned forward to look at me with glowing red eyes, I sat straight up and focused hard on Tanya as she finished making my drink.

"Cheers," she said as she set my drink in front of me.

"Thanks." I leaned forward and took a sip, but Tanya paused.

"Word to the wise, don't go thanking people here," she said, dropping her tone to just above the music. "You can get in a lot of trouble if you owe the wrong person a favor."

At the look of confusion on my face, she shook her head. "Ask whoever got you access to The Crossroads. Clearly, they didn't prepare you enough."

The bartender turned to another customer flagging her down, and she left me with that charming warning and the rest of my mojito. I sighed through my nose and pulled the business card out again. Maybe this had been a mistake. I clearly wasn't learning anything here other than the fact that monsters were real. Which, to be fair, I guess I already knew.

"Hello there, pretty thing."

I turned, taking the last sip of my drink, fully expecting this to be a nearby conversation. But when I turned to find three pairs of yellow eyes on me, I set my glass down. Two big masculine figures and a very feminine one were watching me. One of the guys had spoken to me. His hair slicked back and his chest trying to pop out of a t-shirt two sizes too small. He looked for all the world like an actor, or athlete, or something else equally glamorous.

"Hello?"

That earned me three smiles, mostly friendly looking, save for the fangs that caused me to stiffen.

"Easy on the human, Rex." Tanya came to my end of the bar, leaning forward and letting the end of her gold chain pool on the marble surface. "She's new."

Rex smirked, not a malicious thing but with amusement and intrigue. "Oh, I can tell. I'd remember a face like that."

"And that set of tits," the woman beside him chimed in, licking her lips before moving her gaze up towards my face.

"Show us what those legs can do on the dance floor, pretty thing?" Rex asked.

I ran my tongue along my teeth, thinking. Tanya leaned in to whisper, "He's one of the good ones. They really do just want to dance with you. Maybe a snack if you feel like parting with some blood, but they take 'no' for the answer it is."

Nodding, I slid off my stool and slid Tanya the cash for my drink, plus a tip. If I had ever needed to let loose a bit and forget my problems with a sexy group of, well, whatever they were, it would be now.

"Sure thing, Rex. Why don't you show me what they offer at The Crossroads?"

# Chapter Eleven

## Zendrax

I was a fool. A fool to keep Henri's company when I was the most loathsome creature in this or any realm. Sitting in the recess of a taller tower in Old Town, I watched Henri's window. I vowed to keep watch over that building, and I would do it, even when my muddled heart couldn't handle being atop it.

There was one existence for me. One. Atone for my failures by doing good in the name of my fallen clan. My priority would forevermore be repentance. My baser needs would always be second, and minimal. And with my mourning period over, I had barely begun doing small tasks that kept me out of sight. Removing broken branches from the roads after a storm. Pulling debris out of the river as I fished for my meals. To seek out affection would be beneath my atonement, wouldn't it? But Henri seemed genuinely glad to have my company. Did my presence stir happiness in her, and if so, did that count as doing good?

The window of warm yellow light that I'd been watching snuffed out. To bed, then. The light had been on all evening, from the dip of the sun and a few hours after. With Henri asleep, I felt better moving away from the building. I had watched this quarter of the city for months, and there was almost nothing lurking here that would be a true danger. What little threat there was, it seemed to have no interest in the buildings I kept to.

Stretching my wings, I let my weight fall from the sunken crevice where I hid, catching the gusts between the buildings to coil a path down to the ground where I could make my way to the river. There were pockets, alleys, and old buildings no longer in use where I could hide my presence as I made my way down to the water.

The grass underfoot was crisp with the evening chill as I climbed down a steep bank of the wide river. It was secluded from the view of any bridges, and I had luck with the fish in this place. Wet, clay-filled soil stained my fingers and claws until I reached the rocky ground at the lapping edge of the river. Just a step or two wide, just enough to bend down and wash my hands before eyeing the dark water for signs of dinner. The glistening surface reflected some stars. Not many, not enough. This place was so filled with light that few were visible. Or perhaps there simply was none to be seen in this realm. Yet another difference for me to adjust to. But I liked looking at them all the same. Even with the name for them, as Henri had said, freckles, the stars still reminded me of her speckled skin.

A dark shadow cutting through the reflection interrupted my gaze. A familiar shape of wings, a long tail, clawed feet. A gargoyle.

I shot to my feet, wings spread and claws at the ready. What was another gargoyle doing here? I had seen none in months, not since I left my own realm. Was there a clan to be had in this place? The Mistress made no mention of it when she told me where I could roost the most comfortably. And surely other gargoyles would house themselves in Old Town where the tall buildings and statues would hide them, wouldn't they?

The figure moved across the sky, too recklessly among this city of humans that shouldn't see us. The figure dipped over a grouping of trees, and I lost sight of the silhouette and swore. Running, I caught the first current I could over the water to swoop up to those trees and follow the shape.

The trees were in a large, cultivated yard with some kind of communal building, like a house of scholars or perhaps a collection of offices. But there were enough of them, thick and strong and old, able to hold my weight. I half-climbed as I reached the biggest one, making my way up into the top branches that would carry me so that I could see. The sky was empty of flight, a cloudless, moon-slivered night that was open and clear enough to see for a great stretch. There was no way it could have gotten so far away that I couldn't see it now, so it must have landed somewhere.

Off. Something was off about this, and I couldn't rest my mind over what I'd seen. I was certain it was another gargoyle, but there were a great many creatures in this realm that were unfamiliar to me. Maybe I spotted something else. There would be only one way to know for sure. I had to speak to The Mistress, or perhaps her aide Stefan. One of them would know the answers I craved.

My descent from the tree was more careful as I kept to the shadows. Slipping out of the yard and into the dark banks of the river, I knew where I had to go.

The Crossroads was as loud as ever. The thrumming noise that this realm used for music was too much for me. It rattled my teeth and agitated my mind as I pulled the door spelled to open only for the ones approved by The Mistress. The alley was dark and empty as I slipped inside and went down the stairs.

The scents assaulted me, sweat and alcohol among the mix of creatures and bodies. I swept into the room and towards the bar when a hint of something else entirely crossed my senses. Henri? I looked around. No, no, Henri was in her home. I watched her lights go out. She was simply on my mind so much the past few days that I was imagining it. Pressing forward, I found one of the golden-collared -servants behind the bar. Topping a drink with a yellow fruit and sliding it to a fae before turning to me, surprised.

"I'd heard we had a gargoyle in the city," she said. "What can I get you?"

"I need to speak with . . ." That scent again. I whipped my head around the space but couldn't find where it was coming from. An agitated growl rattled through me, startling a few of the surrounding patrons.

"Everything alright, big guy?" she asked.

"That scent, I . . ." My hands flexed, open and closed in an anxious tic. I changed what I was going to say entirely. "Are there humans here?"

That was it. It had to be. I wasn't smelling Henri in particular; it was the scent of humans. Henri was simply the only one I had smelled the closest since coming here. The humans of this realm all had that sweetness to them.

"Actually, you just missed one who had a drink." The demoness eyed me with suspicion. "You do remember The Mistress's rules, right? You can't do anything to her without her consent."

I scowled. "I would never. What did she look like? A female, soft and round with red hair and stars on her skin?"

The barkeeper's eyebrows raised high. "You know her? Are you the one who got her access to The Crossroads?"

I didn't know. I wasn't sure. I knew Stefan had spoken to her and made some kind of bargain. There was some vague mention of allowing her into the spaces of monsters, but I hadn't paid close enough attention to it. My world spun around the meal and company I kept that night with Henri, but the details about Stephan's visit were hazy at best.

"Where is Henri?" I asked.

The barkeep nodded her head towards a wall at the far end of the space, one I had ignored where the thrumming music was loudest. "She might still be that way. I'm warning you, though, don't cause any trouble. You don't want me to call for Ivor, or worse, The Mistress."

I pushed away from the bar and was already stalking towards the crowded, drumming part of the space. There were many creatures, many bodies moving with the waves and crashes of the music. It was strange, yet satisfying to watch the intimate touches, the gazes that made silent promises to their partners. But where was . . .

Bodies parted enough as one song ended and another began. I saw her, that flash of hair, the familiar shape of her. More of her skin showed than I had the pleasure of seeing before, and it mesmerized me. The thin, short tunic she wore exposed a delicious expanse of skin that I could run a hand around. A slight brushing upward would allow access to her heavy breasts. The pants—no, shorts—that she wore were little more than painted to her skin as I watched the round of her ass move with her dancing. The very act was hypnotic. She was facing away from me. Should I call out to her? Reach for her? Or was she perhaps upset at the way I left things? She had every right to be.

The conflict inside me toiled for a moment until I watched the soft graze of a hand down a lock of her hair. Another female, one of the blood-eaters, was dancing so close to Henri. And that laugh, that musical trill that it drew out of her, clawed at my chest. I wanted to roar, though, at who or why I couldn't begin to explain. All I knew was that the female so near Henri irked me.

But there were more. Two males, more of their sharp-toothed kind, were moving alongside Henri and the female.

This would not do. I was pressing my way through the crowd before I realized it, my wings willing the bodies to part and make space.

I reached out one hand, the lightest of touches, as I had to be careful that my claws would not hurt her delicate skin. Running a knuckle down her arm, I called to her over the beat of the music.

"Henri."

She whirled around, surprised. Her face flushed from moving her body, and her lips rounded into a call of surprise that I couldn't hear over the thrumming room.

"Hey, don't just put your hands on her," one of the males started, but Henri made her intentions clear the moment her eyes landed on me.

"Zendrax!" she called, flinging her arms around me. I had to duck as she practically jumped up, wrapping her arms around my neck.

"You are not upset with me?" I asked, even as I moved my arms to hold her. Everywhere her skin touched me was fire against my stone. The smell of her was intoxicating, and I breathed deeply into her cloud of hair to catch more of it. I may never have my fill of her scent.

"If you're not dancing, move!" someone called near us.

Turning, I glared at the male with horns like a bull, but Henri pulled at my hands and placed them on her hips. My fingers squeezed on reflex, and her face flushed as she smiled, then moved. I knew it for what this realm called dancing, or at least what dancing was to be done at The Crossroads. It was nothing like any dance I knew from Stoneforge, but when Henri did it, it was magic. Unafraid to allow our bodies to brush against one another, she turned to place her supple backside against me as she moved, keeping her hands over mine to ensure they stayed on her hips.

Her face overflowed with delight, and I almost dared hope it was for me. But it could be for the music, the dancing, the alcohol that lightly scented her, or any number of other things. And yet, I couldn't stop myself from the thought. In the end, all that mattered in that moment was the entwining of our movements as I ignored the thrumming music and let everything from Henri wash over me. Her scent, her hair that brushed against my abdomen as she moved, her touch on my hands, her backside brushing the front of my kilt. Groaning, I could feel the strain of my cock as it began to harden, but I pushed the thoughts away. This was a disservice to my starry-faced human.

Whether she heard the sound that I'd just made or otherwise simply decided in that moment to turn her head, the sight of her impish smile struck me. "I'm glad you're here."

Moving my fingers, I squeezed her hips, digging ever so lightly into her with my claws to let her feel the pressure without hurting her. A tremor ran down her body, and she looked at me with wide, topaz eyes. I wanted to shatter. I was so overfilled with emotions now that I had Henri in my grasp.

When the song ended and a new bombardment of sounds began, Henri gently pulled me off the dance floor. "Let's go talk. I can't believe this is where I found you."

Talk. She wanted to talk. I was happy to let the small woman pull me off the dancing area and to one of the silk-draped alcoves. She still wanted to talk to me, even after leaving the way I did. Henri let go of my hand when we reached one of the secluded spots, nothing but a sofa and a low table in front of it with odd cuffs at each corner. Restraints for sexual pleasure of some kind or another, I was sure. That's what this place seemed to be for. So, that begs the question, why was Henri here?

She sat on the sofa, nodding for me to sit next to her. Testing the structure, I felt satisfied enough to put my weight on it. This place was, after all, made for all sorts of creatures.

"I was worried about you," Henri admitted.

My hand moved, and suddenly I was cupping her cheek. My thumb moved across her delicate skin, stopping as I brushed her bottom lip. "Never waste your worries on me. I am only . . ."

Only what? A banished gargoyle. A truth I had butted up against and yet never revealed to Henri. How much of my turmoil stemmed from this? From not being truthful to her?

"A what?" Her hand moved over mine, still cupping her cheek. "Please talk to me, Zen."

The air caught in my chest with a hiss.

"You would use a piece of my name?" I asked. "This is a name of affection?"

"Do you not like it? I don't have to," she said.

"No, I do like it. I like it very much."

She smiled, then it fell. "I don't like how we left things."

My chest rumbled somewhere between a growl and a purr. "Neither do I. Let me make you another promise, Henri. I swear to you that I will tell you only truths."

That brought a dazzling smile to her face, and then from the alcove next to ours we heard the first moan. Accompanied by a wet, slick sound. Henri's face flushed, even as she hid her broad grin.

"I, um," she cleared her throat, even as the next hot, wet sound interrupted her. "I didn't know you were into this sort of place."

"I am not. Gargoyles are rarely promiscuous creatures. When we find a bedmate, we remain together for a long time." I moved my hand from her cheek, though I didn't want to, and placed it on my knee for lack of a better restraint on myself. Stars, she was gloriously enticing. Everything about Henri drew me to her, and I was starting to think it had nothing to do with

101

her being the first person I had truly interacted with in months. If that were the case, I would have been just as interested in Stefan or the barkeep or the other dancers.

"I can't take it, Sir. Please, put it in!" The mewling cry came from the next secluded compartment. There was no debating what was going on, and Henri slapped a hand over her mouth to muffle her amusement.

It was good that the moment entertained Henri, but the sounds from the next booth, and the scents of this place, only made me keenly aware of her. My jaw clenched as it hit me, my eyes dropping from her face to the curve of her body, the round of her breasts and thighs. The reaction I had from seeing her in this place, dancing with those other creatures. I didn't covet Henri as my first friend. I wanted more, and I shouldn't.

"What's wrong?" Her face turned to concern quickly as she studied me.

"Nothing," I rumbled. It came out hoarse and rushed, and I knew from the look on her face she didn't believe me. "I am sorry, only truths. It is this place. There are too many distractions to my senses here."

A wet sucking sound from next to us had me clenching my fists. This was not helping. The thin drape of black silk was a mere pretense of privacy. Hells, I could lean forward and see right into their space if I so desired. Whatever they were doing, they were enjoying it. Audibly.

"Are you here for sexual gratification?" I asked. I wasn't sure if it was appropriate, but there was no avoiding the subject.

It was quite literally all around us, and the question had been driving me wild.

Her face flushed, those plump lips tightening into a thin line. "No." It came out as barely more than a whisper. "I was hoping to find out more about you."

Oh.

She nibbled on her lower lip for a minute, looking around The Crossroads. "This is ridiculous, isn't it?"

Another moan from our neighbors.

I couldn't hold back the smile. "It is."

"Do you want to go back to my apartment? It would be easier to talk there."

Henri. Soft, kind, talented Henri. Forgiving Henri.

"If you would have me, I would be honored."

That earned me a smile. A real, dazzling smile from her as she stood, smoothing out the small scrap of clothing that acted as her tunic. "Perfect. I'll order a car and meet you back there as soon as I can."

I tilted my head, studying her. "There is no need, Henri. I can take us back right now."

She raised an eyebrow. "How?"

Standing, I watched the movement of her hips as she stepped aside to make room for my larger form to stand beside her. My claws itched to feel her weight in my hands. If she'd allow me to carry her. It was so wrong for me to want anything but my atonement, and yet the idea of sharing my wings with her was too tempting.

"You'll see."

# Chapter Twelve

## Henri

Nothing like a lungful of crisp night air to help your screams echo off the buildings.

"It is alright, Henri. I have you."

Arms wrapped tightly around Zendrax's neck, my eyes widened with terror as he lifted us off the ground. I can't believe I didn't realize sooner what he had in mind. But the moment we were in the alley and out of the club, he picked me up as if I wasn't two good fistfuls of curvy lady, and we were already taking off. The door to the club disappeared all too soon, and then we landed on the top of the building for a moment for Zen to adjust his wings, I think.

"Zendrax—"

"Zen," he insisted, which was really fucking cute, except this wasn't the time for that.

"*Zen*, I regret to inform you that I'm now terrified of *heights*!"

Before the last word could leave my mouth, he had covered the expanse of the building in two gliding leaps. Then we were back in the air, even higher than before. My arms tightened around his neck, and I squeezed my eyes shut. My heart was hammering in my chest with every dip and flap of those huge wings. I knew in my heart that flying was not for me, and that my fat ass would have been happier on the ground than in the air.

"Henri," Zen's voice rumbled next to my ear. "You are with me. I will not drop you."

"I'm scared of heights!" I squeaked, burying my face into his neck. "Please put me on the ground!"

Big arms snaked around my ribs and under my ass as he held me tighter. "As you wish, Henri."

Thank fucking God.

With every gust that had us veering from one side or the other I had to bite back a scream. I kept my eyes sealed shut. They stayed that way until finally, *finally,* I felt it as we landed. Shifting my weight in his arms, I could tell he was standing on solid ground.

On a quiet street, we stopped under a broken streetlight, offering Zendrax the most cover. Not that many people would be up right now, and it seemed to be a quiet residential street. The gargoyle placed me on my feet, but as he found me still shaky, he scooped me back up into his arms.

"You are afraid."

"No, I'm still calming down." But I couldn't argue too much. I knew why he would think that from my expression and my voice. "Thank you for putting me down."

"I am sorry, Henri." He leaned down and pressed his forehead to mine. "I wanted to share my wings with you, but I had no idea you would be so afraid. You climbed on the roof that night, so I thought you wouldn't mind."

Pulling my coat tighter, I laid my head against him. "It's fine. I can stand now."

Once I was on my feet again, I flexed my fingers, trying to shake off the strain of clutching to Zendrax for dear life. Reaching up to the semblance of a ponytail I'd put my hair in, I yanked out the scrunchie and slipped it over my wrist to scratch my too-tight scalp.

"Do you know how to get back from here? Is it too far to walk, or should I get a car?"

"Not too far," he said as he hovered. It was almost cute to see the worry on his face. "Seven crossed streets from here."

"Seven blocks?" My eyebrows jumped upward, and I whipped my head toward home. "You can fly so fast."

"Not fast," he corrected. "To fly straight to my destination is much quicker than moving through the cars and around the buildings, as you do."

"That makes sense." I stared at the buildings just over the tops of the townhouses we stood by now. Old Town was nearly in sight, or at least one or two of the highest spires were visible.

"Do you like flying?" I asked. "Isn't it scary to think you could fall? What happens if your wings cramp up or something?"

"They haven't before. That is a problem for fledglings." Zen crouched down next to me, taking one of my hands and placing it on the hard outer ridge of his wing. "My wings will never fail me."

He flexed it, and I jumped at the feel of hard cords under my palm. Tendons, or sinew, or whatever made up the contents of a gargoyle, shifted under my touch at his movement. Zendrax looked wholly amused by my reaction.

"I will not break apart, Henri. Especially when carrying such a precious passenger." My heart skipped as his tone dropped to say it, clear intent in his voice. Licking dry lips, I studied that face. Closer now than I'd gotten since that night in my apartment. The shape of him, the lines of his face and the curves of his chest and arms. He lifted me like I weighed nothing, a sensation I'd never felt before. That tail swished by his feet, and it caught my eye for just long enough to remind me how different we were.

Zendrax was definitely not human, but the more I spent time with him, the more those differences fell away. When I looked at him, I just saw Zendrax, not a gray guy with wings and horns. But it didn't stop me from wanting to kiss—

My hand flew to cover my mouth. *Where did that come from?*

Okay, yes, it didn't come from nowhere. Hot as sin with a horse cock. Early on, I'd obviously had that thought, even just out of morbid curiosity. But this? Kissing him? That was new. Maybe it was just the fleeting ambiance from The Crossroads. Or maybe it was the man in front of me that had saved me, spoken kind words to me, was genuinely joyous for my company.

"What's wrong?" he asked, brow furrowed.

"Nothing." I took my hand from my face. Ok, we needed to talk. That was the whole point of this trip to my apartment, to sort out our shit. "I can walk back. I'll meet you there. I guess you don't want to be walking around where people can see you, huh?"

"If you would allow me, I will offer to fly us there." Zen held out a hand, tilting his head. "I know you have fears, and I understand them, so I won't ask you to overcome them for me. But whenever you would have me, I will always be willing to share my wings with you."

My chest was tight and warm. "Zen. Thank you." Eyeing the distant towers of Old Town, I cringed. "I'll keep it in mind, but not tonight."

He nodded. "I understand, then I will watch over you as you walk back."

"Thank you." After a quick smile, he leapt into the dark sky.

Seven blocks wasn't so bad. At least the shoes I'd picked for the club weren't my *most* uncomfortable heels. Once I realized I had lost track of my gargoyle, I spotted him peeking over a rooftop just ahead of me. Laughing, it became a game of him slipping out of sight and me trying to find him again.

Never before had I felt so safe walking in the middle of the night in the city. Crossgate had its problems, just like any city did, but knowing that my gargoyle was watching over me, I had nothing to fear.

Once I was finally back at the building, Zendrax flew up to the roof to wait for me to open the window. Up the elevator, I finally turned my key in the door of my apartment and sighed as I shut the door.

There he was at my window, perched and watching as I flicked on the lights. It felt good to be home, but more than that, it felt good to have desired company here. I couldn't lie. There had been plenty of lonely times since moving out of my childhood home. Hell, there were lonely times before I ever moved out, but it wasn't the time to focus on that.

Kicking off my shoes as I walked to the window, I pressed my hand against the glass near the latch that would let the panes swing so Zendrax could enter. A large gray hand mirrored mine outside the window, endlessly careful not to scratch the glass. His eyes lit up at my smile, and I opened the latch to let him in.

"Come on in." I moved back to let him find a comfortable place to sit, then chewed on the inside of my cheek, watching him study the available seats. "I need to get you a chair, don't I?"

Zen offered a crooked smile, then sat on a bit of rug next to the unlit fireplace and leaned against it, careful of his wings. "I am used to being wary of human furniture. Don't worry about that."

Finding a spot on the floor next to him highlighted our difference in size. He looked so relaxed, leaning against the brick of the fireplace with his head tilted to watch me. Those jade eyes were intense, settling on me with the focus that he gave everything he looked at. I'd noticed it before, when he first looked around my apartment, but it had stayed consistent since then.

Filling my lungs, I sighed through my nose. "I don't like that things got so weird between us."

"Neither do I," Zendrax admitted.

"Why did you leave?" It was a question that I'd asked myself so many times. "Was it because of me?"

"No," he blurted. "I was not you, it was me. I had . . ." He steeled his jaw, squaring his shoulders. "My thoughts were drifting not toward my mission, but toward my feelings for you."

"Mission?" It wasn't what I expected at all. "Wait, feelings?" Heat crept up my neck, and I couldn't look him in the eyes, suddenly shy. I'd had it all wrong this whole time. I never chased Zen away with my dirty thoughts or my insistence on his visits. It was something else that settled over him that chased him away. A sadness. I could see it now, and it felt like he was ready to open up. "Zen, I think you need to start at the beginning. Tell me everything. How did you come here, and why?"

# Chapter Thirteen
## Zendrax

Henri settled in while I collected my thoughts. She lit the fireplace with supplies she kept near it, and I watched so I would know how she would like it done in the future. I studied the scrunch of her nose when she concentrated, recalling our first meeting. Henri deserved to know everything, and tonight I would tell her.

"There." She sat back down, settling where she could lean against me and still look up as I spoke to her.

My body was stiff as I cleared my throat. "I am banished from my people," I started. Beginning with the most difficult things to say would make the rest easier, or at least I'd hoped.

"Banished?" She rubbed a soothing hand on my knee, a soft, affectionate motion. It gave me the courage to keep going.

"When the leading family of a clan fails that clan, they are delt with swiftly and harshly. My family failed Stoneforge, failed our clan. *I* failed my clan." I started at the battle that ambushed Stoneforge Castle at the break of nightfall. My mother's crumbled body was still fresh in my memory. My sisters that fell; I never did manage to lay eyes on their pieces. By now, they and the rest of the fallen from the battle would be resting in the grassy fields where we laid stones to rest among the moon lilies. There was no chance for me to pay my respects to them, nor did I feel I deserved that honor. Not for the disgraced son that I was.

"What happened to them? To your clan and your family?" Henri asked.

Difficult as it was to get out, I took a deep breath and began. I told her of my clan and my fallen mother and sisters. My uncle's heartbreaking arrival to the fight, the decimation of our home, and Marzav's plan to summon The Mistress. Henri, who had been listening with wide, attentive eyes, stopped to ask several questions at that. Once I sated her curiosity for The Mistress, I told her the rest. My atonement, the ending of my mourning period in which I sought no company or comforts. The empty feeling of my family's absence eases some with time and the ending of the mourning period, but my atonement is incomplete. I must continue to seek out deeds for the betterment of my new realm while I reflect on my failures.

Henri listened to every word. I hadn't felt so understood since leaving my home realm. To live in this strange place and spend my time observing their foreign ways has been hard. Nothing a Stoneforge warrior couldn't handle, but harder than expected. Until a light shone into my night, and her name was Henri.

"You're not alone anymore," Henri soothed, rubbing a hand on my arm with the lightest touch. "I'm so sorry you went through all that. Thank you for telling me."

"Thank you for listening," I answered. "If, someday, you wish to tell me of your clan and family, I would gladly listen."

With a sigh, she leaned her head onto my arm, wrapping her own arms around my biceps. We shared a quiet moment, enjoying the subtle sounds of the crackling logs in the fireplace and the cars on the streets below. "There's not much to tell," Henri broke the silence. "I wanted to be an artist, but it wasn't what my parents wanted for me. My parents and my sister don't understand it and, therefore, don't respect it."

"Is it a requirement of this realm to take up the profession of one's family?" I asked.

Henri snorted. "No, but some parents are just like that, I guess. I still see them on occasion, but I keep it short. If they start harassing me, I leave. I learned a hard lesson when I left home to pursue art."

Mulling over her words, my brows knit together. "But you are an artist. You create art. It is everywhere in your home."

"Ha! I wish Mom saw it that way. I'm hoping to win this competition to help prove it to her. Or me, maybe me. Or maybe I just want the prize money, so I'm not so stressed about bills." Her smile faltered. "No, I do want to shove it in her face. Thankfully, my friends Simon and Chloe have been there for me. I'd love it if you could meet them someday. I guess they're my clan." She smiled. "The ones I chose for myself, anyway."

My brows lowered as I recalled the rules of the realm given to me by The Mistress. "I am unsure if I can add them to the list of people I can reveal my existence to, but I will speak with The Mistress."

A laugh bubbled up from beside me, and I turned to see the joy on her face. "You don't have to do that. I'm not sure how well they'd handle monsters. Ignorance is bliss in this case, I think. Then again," she mused, and a devious look crossed her face, "I might be able to bargain with that Stefan guy. I already added them in with my protections, and I think I created a loophole."

My clever, brilliant stars. Patting the top of Henri's head, I pictured the stiff demon's face as he might look negotiating with Henri. "If you decide to do such a thing, I only beg that you allow me to watch."

"Deal." Henri chuckled, then sighed. She moved from her seat next to me, and I watched the round of her backside as she walked to the kitchen. "This calls for tea and snacks. Are you hungry?"

"I am," I admitted, though more in passing as I watched in wonder at her movements. The amount of understanding she was capable of. The fact that she wasn't ashamed to be near me was a gift I hadn't wholly expected. I felt a shared sadness with her, but knowing that her family did not support her goals also made me angry on her behalf. My strong, shining Henri.

She brought over two steaming mugs and a box of what she called, "leftover pizza." Once she settled the food beside us on the floor, Henri pulled a blanket over and curled up right against me. Her touch was fire on my side, bliss of a kind I hadn't expected, and didn't deserve, but I couldn't help but to let it continue. I curled my tail behind her and then along her leg, as if to press her closer to me. She jumped, then laughed and began to stroke it affectionately.

"So, are you ready to talk about those feelings?" she asked, barely audible over the fire.

"Henri." I gently moved her to face me and urged her chin up with my knuckle. "I care for you. There is nothing to hide from me. I told you the shame of my banishment. There's nothing you could tell me that would make me not want to be here with you."

"Shit." She shook her head, but at least her gaze met mine once again. "This isn't how I wanted this to go. Let me collect myself."

The smile on her face eased my tension. "You asked about my feelings for you. I'll admit to you now that I care for you as a companion, and I am mesmerized by you as a wonderful, talented, curious, beautiful person."

"Companion," she repeated, and I thought for a moment her expression was strained, but she carried it into such a bright smile that I must have imagined it. "I'm glad to be your companion, Zen. Actually, I'm relieved. For a while there, I thought I was bothering you and I had chased you away."

"Never," I said. "I am pleased to be able to speak with you, and to enter your home. You have been most kind to me, and I will sit for as many days as you wish for your drawings."

Henri burst into a laugh at that. "Be careful, or I'll take you up on that." Her laughter calmed, leaving her with a softer smile. "Yeah, I'll take it. I do like you, Zen. I want to keep hanging out."

My chest rumbled with a pleased sound. "Then our sentiments are the same?"

Henri laughed, pulling the blanket around her shoulders and laying against me. "Yeah, Zen. I like you, and it sounds like you like me too. I'm glad we're on the same page."

We talked, deep into the late hours, much to my delight. Everything from gargoyles to her art, to pizza, which she assured me was even better when it was hot. The weight of it all, my banishment, my home, my family, it all lightened when I opened up to my stars. Suddenly, the dark clouds I carried with me all these months cleared enough to breathe. My past wasn't gone, but it no longer consumed me with guilt when I thought about what Henri would think of me. I was foolish to not give her more credit, because she was willing to accept me despite it all.

The night drifted by, and as her yawns became frequent and her eyelids became heavy, I eventually left to seek a rooftop to sun for the encroaching daytime. I left through her window after she pried a promise out of me to see her again, noting that she didn't latch the window after me. I perched on the rooftop opposite her window so that I could look on as the daylight took me and let my thoughts roll around inside my head.

Could I do good in the world and still keep Henri at my side? I could try. I'd have to try, because at this point there was no moving on from her. I growled as I reflected on the winged figure that caught my attention as it passed over me at the river. Whatever it was, I would ensure it couldn't encroach on my domain. Old Town, and the starry-faced goddess that lived within it, were mine to protect.

# Chapter Fourteen

## Zendrax

My senses came to me as the warmth of the sun receded. A sigh came to me first, and I was rewarded with the sight of Henri hard at work in her room, her lip pouty and her nose scrunched, as she chipped away at a sculpture. I spent my last two nights with Henri, talking and enjoying her company much as we had done that first night. I longed to go to her again, and yet the shadowy figure I saw in the sky sat ill within my mind. Tonight was not for Henri, not yet. Not until I at least tried to find out more. The moment the sun released me from its grasp, I spread my wings and took to the shadows, making my way to The Crossroads.

The more time I spent with one of the humans of Crossgate City, the more comfortable I became. Henri had already pointed out areas where I could move debris or remove refuse for good deeds. And flying over the streets now held more importance than the mindless crossing of humans and their vehicles. Now there were places Henri had pointed out to me that she liked to go, there were the streets she had walked on the way back to her home from The Crossroads. There were even places that now held memories for me by association, such as the pizza shop with the illuminated image that matched the one on the top of the box we ate from together. Henri tinted everything, and it brought new light into my world.

I landed in the alley that would let me walk down to The Crossroads, avoiding the humans just around the corner that were lined up for the upper level that concealed the truly monstrous place below. Down the stairs, the scents and sounds of lust hit me, and I grumbled as I willed my cock not to imagine Henri in her terribly short tunic and shorts, like the last time I was here.

The more causes I had to come to this place, the more familiar I grew. The golden collared ones who worked for The Mistress were easy for me to spot now, and I approached one behind the bar.

"I would like to speak to The Mistress," I said.

A curvaceous deer-legged woman offered a warm smile as she propped her elbows on the bar. "You're going about it the wrong way, friend. Do you have some sort of appointment with her? A deal? She doesn't like to be bothered when she's having playtime."

As if on cue, a scream erupted from down the hallway of phallic sconces and playroom doors. The fawn grinned. "And right now, she is very much in the middle of playtime."

I sighed, unsure what to do next, when her assistant came to mind. "Is Stefan available in her stead?"

She nodded. "That I can work with. One moment."

The woman disappeared behind the bar, coming up a moment later with a notepad. "Write your name on here and he'll see it. That will let him know who's here to see him, and if he chooses to meet with you, you'll see him soon."

An odd practice, but no more strange than any of the other magics I've seen performed by the beings of The Crossroads. I took the paper and a writing implement, inspecting the item that wasn't a quill or charcoal stick for a moment before writing my name on the paper. The letters changed as I wrote them, shaping themselves into a foreign tongue I hadn't seen in this realm before, and then glowed before disappearing as though sinking into the paper.

"While you wait, can I get you anything? Beer? Wine? Blood?"

"None, I will wait for Stefan."

"Good luck," she offered, and nearly turned to the next patron when a question occurred to me.

"Wait, have you seen another of my kind?" I asked. "A gargoyle in this city?"

"Have I seen a gargoyle before?" She thought for a moment. "Some creatures with wings, sure, but a gargoyle? No, I don't think so."

Disappointment at the lack of a clue struck me, but it was not the fawn's fault. "Your answer is appreciated, tavern keeper. I won't intrude on your business any longer."

She gave me a nod, then moved to the next person in need of her attentions.

I moved to a nearby wall, keeping my back to it as I watched the room. I didn't like not having the vantage point of a rooftop on my side, but I could at least remain watchful of the room. It was only a few moments later that a puff of smoke at my elbow had me looking down into the eyes of the demon himself.

"Hello again, Zendrax the gargoyle. What can I do for you today?" Stefan asked.

"I am concerned about something else living in this city. I was hoping you could tell me more." I rolled my shoulders, my stiff wings glad that I moved off the wall to face the demon.

"There are a great many things living in this city. You'll have to give me details," Stefan answered. "But let's go this way, and I'll speak with you in the sitting room."

I followed Stefan, not to the hallway as I had last time, but to a small concealed door to the side. It opened into a rather modest room, considering the rest of the building, and I found myself on a sturdy black couch facing opposite a matching one that Stefan was now seated on. A marble coffee table between us was the only proper furniture to be found, though the art on the wall reminded me of exactly what carnal acts went on behind the closed doors of this place.

"Before we begin, I will warn you that some creatures who live here I cannot speak of with you. Confidentiality clauses, you see. It all depends on who has a deal with whom."

I nodded. "Anything you can say is appreciated. My concerns are with another gargoyle in the city."

Stefan's expression darkened. "Another gargoyle, you say? I'd have to consult the books to see if any have come through our channels, but I don't recall a gargoyle besides yourself. As for gargoyles already living in Crossgate City, I cannot recall any who contracted with us in the past few hundred years, though I'm sure a few have come and gone through other channels in that time. Your kind simply does not dwell here in the modern age."

I furrowed my brow, staring into the void between us as I remembered the figure. "It could fly, and it was around my size. I may have confused the shape in the dark, but the wings were unmistakable. What else could it be?"

"If there is a gargoyle, it would have to have come through a portal that was not ours." Stefan brushed his fingers down his breast pocket, tilting his head. "I suppose I could look into it for you, at the price of a small boon, of course."

Frowning, I looked the demon up and down. "I do not know what a boon would cost me. The Mistress has yet to call upon me for the boon I owe her, and that has not sat well with me either."

Stefan held out his hand and summoned his ledger in a puff of smoke, flipping to a specific page. "Yes, you're correct. It looks like she was gracious enough to wait for you to get settled, but I actually think we've had a matter to be settled and were looking for the right person for the job. Yes, yes, you might do nicely."

He closed the book and sent it away with a snap and another whisper of smoke. "I'll ask her tonight, and we'll be in touch. I'll see if I can get this boon off of your shoulders, and if you can get a thorn out of our side in the process. And if I happen to learn anything of your mystery gargoyle, I'll even pass it on at a steep discount. What do you think?"

I hesitated, but there was no deal struck between us. I also wished to be rid of my obligation to The Mistress . . .

"I agree to your terms," I answered. "Let's see what The Mistress has to say."

# Chapter Fifteen

## Henri

"And this is the last one." I hefted up a carved bowl onto the counter at Magical Muse, Rita clapping in delight.

"That one! That's the one that will sell first," she insisted. Picasso purred as he rolled himself between my feet, belly-up.

"You think so?" I grinned.

"She's right," Chloe added. "That one's special."

The bowl in question was one of several pieces I'd made in the last handful of days. It would seem that repairing my relationship with Zendrax had boosted my enthusiasm for carving. I'd made a set of bookends, a handful of soapstone animals that I'd carved while talking to Zen, and this bowl inspired by koi fish swimming in a pond which would make a great birdbath. I wouldn't admit to Simon that I was practicing fluid, soft lines after what he said about the mayor's tastes, but that might have been a little bit of my inspiration.

"You've already got them tagged?" Rita asked, jotting down the pieces in the ledger.

"Already priced and marked," I confirmed. "Hopefully, the arts festival will bring some feet through here to buy them up."

"Are you participating this year?" Rita asked. "I've got a stool and a spot right outside the window if you want to carve in real time. A jazz duo from the music academy is going to set up right at the corner, too. It's going to be a blast."

I smiled. "I might, but I don't know how well I would do with that many eyes on me while I work."

"It's fine! You'll forget they're even there," Chloe said. "I brought out that tree-shaped headboard and stained all the leaves different colors last year, remember? It doesn't take much to entertain the crowd. They're half full of beers from the bar on the corner, anyway. I'll even help you carry one of your big rocks in my cart." She patted the very wagon she'd lent me to bring pieces to Muse today.

"I'll think about it, I swear. I still need to figure out my plan for the Centennial Celebration Art Contest, and that has to come first."

"Still?" Chloe frowned. "Can I do anything to help?"

"Inspiration will strike when you're not looking for it," Rita cut in. "Let it go. Let the universe flow through you and tell you what it wants you to create."

Chloe rolled her eyes, but I smiled at Rita. "Thanks, I'll try to keep myself open to the universe."

"Wise choice." Rita nodded. "Hey, do you kids want to stay for yoga and goats? We're setting up out back in a little while."

"Yoga and goats?" Chloe deadpanned.

"Yeah! My soul-sibling is bringing some babies from their farm while we do an intermediate session. I have extra mats."

"I'll pass, Rita. I want to get back home before it gets dark," I said.

"I have a piece to finish for a client," Chloe said by way of answer, then narrowed her eyes at me. "Why do you need to be home before dark? Is this a newly imposed curfew for yourself?"

My heart skipped, and I couldn't keep the grin off my face. "Something like that."

"I know for a fact you don't wake up before noon, so why go home so early?" Chloe asked.

"Just really focusing on art, I guess." I shrugged. Zendrax counted as art, right? He could have all my focus after sundown.

She shook her head. "Whatever you say. Maybe tonight will be the night inspiration hits you."

"Ugh." I made a face. "One can only hope."

I finished up with Rita before Chloe and I parted ways at Muse. She took her wagon with her, folding it up and waiting at the bus stop where I made sure she wasn't alone until her bus arrived. The wait wasn't long, but she peppered me with probing questions I did my best to avoid. It wasn't quite time to try the whole 'gargoyles are real' thing with her again. Not yet.

Riding high from dropping off so many pieces at the shop and collecting a little bit from some prints that sold was a successful start to the evening as I quickly made it back home to my block, stopping at the corner market on my way. I grabbed everything I needed to make breakfast for dinner. Eggs, pancake mix, bacon, potatoes. I'd learned early on just how much Zen could eat, so I wanted to be prepared for an absolute feast if he came by tonight. If not, I'd be ready for him tomorrow.

Up the stairs, and off the elevator, I juggled my bags and my keys inside. With everything put away, I shifted gears to cleaning up the dusty aftermath of the past few days and the finished pieces that came out of them. Eventually, the place was clean and stocked. I hopped in the shower after a busy day, and to my disappointment, the red glow of the sun still greeted me upon my exit.

I fell onto my bed with a sigh. The sunset was sure taking its time. Rolling over onto my side, I stared at my nightstand for a moment before my eyes landed on the drawer. I considered my recent filthy, *filthy* state of mind for about half a second before pulling open the drawer and retrieving Buzz. Sleek, purple, and fully charged. If I took care of myself now, could I keep my filthy thoughts away from Zen later? Hopefully, because I had to try something before I made a move and had the poor guy uncomfortable again.

Companions, he said. I could respect that, could even enjoy that. Zen was good company, and I wouldn't ruin that. He may have protested that our first encounter with my hand and his cock wasn't what drove him away before, but that had to be part of it, right? Look at the way he frowned and looked away when I flashed my panties by accident. Not that it stopped me from meeting him most nights in my usual t-shirt and nothing else, but I'd been trying to keep it in check for him. Even tonight, I was wearing a shirt that was way too big for me and came down to my thighs.

But that didn't stop Henri Louise Prichard from having needs. I clicked Buzz to life and clicked through the settings until I found my favorite and pulled my panties to the side. The round head of the vibrator settled between my legs in just the right position against my clit and my head fell back on the pillow. My eyes closed and my free hand moved to my neck. How many times had I felt Zen's hands brush my skin there as he moved my curls out of the way? I loved the feel of his touch. His hands were just rough enough without being abrasive and painful. Other parts of him like his wings were smooth, almost a polished quality to them that was silky to the touch. His touch was all I could focus on as my fingers trailed lightly from my neck, then pulling up my shirt to expose my breasts. What would those big hands feel like here? The most tender parts of me were heated with the thought of it.

The vibrator pressed against me was already slick with arousal. A pulsing sensation paired with imagining his touch on my breasts was making quick work of me as a whimper fell from my lips. I was clenching on nothing, which was a damn shame because now I was wondering how it would feel for something of Zen's thickness to slide into me. Was it even possible? Surely, right? Some people work all the way up to fisting. Some people push whole babies out of there. Surely, I could fit Zen, right?

Dangerous. I was letting my thoughts get dangerous, and a little piece of me felt disgusted with myself for lusting after a friend. But I couldn't stop myself, and his name was pulled from me with the encroaching orgasm as I was pushed higher and higher on that rise before the fall.

"*Zen.*"

Click.

My eyes flew open, and I yanked Buzz away, using both hands to prop myself up on the bed. The sounds of my favorite setting hung in the air as my eyes met a pair of jade ones through the window. The sun was gone, replaced by the early night sky, and one unreadable gargoyle.

# Chapter Sixteen

## Henri

My heartbeat spiked, and I pulled my thighs together as another click emerged from the window. It was his claws at the glass as he moved to open it. I'd stopped latching it days ago, and he knew he could let himself in. I turned Buzz off, all the blood in my body rushing to my face as shame and embarrassment washed away my rising climax.

*So much for being companions, Henri!*

Zen stood inside now, closing the window behind him without letting his eyes leave me. I pulled my legs up against me and hung my head, unable to look at him any longer.

"You must be so disgusted right now." It came out as little more than a whisper, and I could feel the first hot, wet tears forming in my eyes. I held them back, unwilling to let him see me cry. How long could I hold back the tears, though, when I had just ruined the best thing that's happened to me in a long time?

"Look at me, Henri," Zen commanded. I hesitated, but a clawed finger touched the underside of my chin and urged it upward. Searching his expression, I still couldn't read him.

"Aren't you mad at me?" I asked, needing to know how badly I'd messed up.

His brow furrowed. "Why would I be angry with you?"

*Is he really going to make me say it?* "I was masturbating, and I called your name. You must be so uncomfortable right now. And after I chased you away before when I touched you inappropriately!"

His thumb caressed my bottom lip, ending my rambling before it could really get started. His other fingers now curled under my chin, and I leaned ever so lightly into his touch.

"I had no idea you had those thoughts for me," Zen said. "I am banished, disgraced. A gargoyle unworthy to hope for your affections."

I blinked. *Did he say hope?*

"I am undeserving of your attentions, Henri," he said, a solemness in his voice.

It was enough to move me from his hold on my chin as I guided his hand away with mine. "You don't get to decide that for me, Zen. I've—" I swallowed. "I've wanted you from day one. I'm so attracted to you, it's pathetic. And I've been scared to ruin our friendship with my dirty thoughts."

Zen was kneeling by my bed, close enough to feel the slight warmth from the sun he had perched in until a few minutes ago. I wanted to fling my arms around him and beg him to give me another chance. It was selfish to grasp at the hope that he wasn't mad at me, that this could all be forgotten and never spoken of again.

He ran a hand down his face and sighed, ending in a low rumble from his throat. When he looked at me again, his eyes were burning with something. Whatever it was, it wasn't anger, and my heart hit my chest so hard it hurt as I waited with bated breath for him to say something.

Shifting his position, he faced me and moved a hand to either side of me on the bed. I turned to match him, my legs tucked under me and my big shirt covering as much of my thighs as I could.

"You desire me?" he asked.

*Fuck, this is torture.* "Yes."

That rumble from his chest came back, and admittedly the wetness between my thighs wasn't entirely leftovers from before.

"I have wanted to bed you for days now," he admitted, "but I was ashamed. I do not deserve your affections."

I frowned. "What do you mean, you don't deserve my affections?"

"My banishment, the atonement."

That moved me from sitting on my legs to getting up on my knees just to almost match the height of his gaze. Hands on my hips, I scoffed. "What does that have to do with anything?"

He startled at that. "I am undeserving."

"You are no such thing. You are many things, Zendrax of Stoneforge. You are kind, you are gorgeous, you are strong, you are dedicated. You are *not* undeserving. There is so much more to you than this banishment. Your atonement can still be a part of you, but it doesn't have to define you. You're already working on that. Just last night, you pulled a bunch of tires from the river. The night before, you replanted that big-ass tree that had gotten shaken loose from the sewer construction. No one is undeserving of affection."

Zen was silent for a long moment, then he hung his head. "I don't know if you're right or not, Henri, but I can no longer resist you."

It was a gift I didn't expect but also a pain to see him like that, all wrapped up in one. Reaching out a hand to cup his cheek, I at least got him to look at me. "I like you, Zen. A lot. If you like me in that way too, then don't you think we should give it a try?"

He groaned, pressing his cheek into my touch. "Can I kiss you?"

Breaking out into a grin, I nodded, and he moved in like lightning to meet my lips. His kiss was passionate, consuming, and still warm from the sun that he'd sat under all day. My tongue slipped between my lips to taste him. Something salty and almost smoky about him pulled a moan from me as one of his hands moved to my hip and I gasped and the sudden, firm grip.

"You wish to find release?" he asked, moving his mouth from mine and down my neck.

I shivered. "Yes."

"Then you shall find it." He lifted me like I weighed nothing and pulled me closer to the edge of the bed. Panic rose as I worried about my body. Was a human too weird for him? Too squishy? Would he find wetness from arousal unpleasant?

He moved one hand to the base of my neck, not putting pressure around it per se, but definitely using just enough force to urge me to lie back. I complied, but my worries were still there.

"Have you ever seen a naked human before?" I asked.

He was still tall enough that I could see his face, even as he kneeled over the bed. His expression moved to something almost playful. "Yes, I have, and I am positive I will find you to be the most pleasant of all."

In one swift move, he scooted my shirt up my body, revealing everything from bellybutton down for him to see. The pink rose panties I wore weren't exactly lingerie material, but Zen didn't seem to care as he snagged a clawed finger at each hip.

"I'm going to remove what is in my way, understand?"

Nodding, because that's about all I could do when faced with his matter-of-fact tone, I let my knees fall apart enough to not obstruct him. Grasping at my bedding, I wiggled enough to let him slide the panties right off of me as he discarded them on my nightstand.

He leaned over me, closing his eyes as he inhaled. A rumble from his chest had me at his mercy. "You smell delectable, my stars."

Just hearing him call me that made me thankful for the freckles splattered across my skin. Warmth spread through me at his touch, his words, his care, as he moved my knees apart.

"Today's release is yours. You will need to be prepared before I take you."

"Aw!" I protested, but he just chuckled and stroked my cheek.

"I would never risk hurting you, my stars. Allow me to pleasure you and see how much you can handle before we try such a thing. Even in my realm, we knew to do this for human bedmates."

I huffed, but relented as his hand moved down to explore. He gripped a thigh with one hand, letting his thumb pull me open while the other hand was content to run a finger right down the center of me, shocking my clit in the process. Somehow, he did all of this without piercing my soft bits with any claws, and my eyes locked on that shiny wet finger as he lifted it to his mouth and sucked. His eyes closed as he made a satisfactory moan.

"I knew it."

"Knew what?" I whispered.

His eyes opened and settled on me. "You are indeed delicious."

And fuck me if that didn't send a shiver down my back and straight to where I was clenching on nothing again. My legs nudged closed in a search for friction, pressure, anything to ease the feeling, but Zendrax pushed my knees apart again.

"We have barely begun," he crooned. "Allow me to continue."

"Yes, please." It wasn't lost on me that he already had me begging with one look and barely a touch, and I didn't care as long as he kept going.

Zen leaned down, his face so close I could feel his breath as he opened his mouth. I noticed, not for the first time, that he had fangs. But in this context, it sent a thrill through me. His tongue reached forward and licked. I noticed it was more purple than expected, but not unlike a human's in texture, from what I could tell. I cried out in surprise at the pressure he put against my clit, as his warm tongue rolled up and off of me, giving me a look at how long it was.

"Ahh," he rumbled, satisfied. "I see you have a weakness there."

"I wouldn't call it a weakNESS—"

That was no human tongue, that was the tongue of a giraffe. He licked me again, and this time he stayed there. His tongue was a little scratchy, like a cat. Only, with all the arousal dripping from me, there was no pain or rough sensation. I couldn't stop myself as I propped up on my elbows to see what was happening. Zen's head between my thighs was so erotic, the image of it so surreal as he allowed himself long strokes with his tongue. It wasn't long before he began changing his motions. Spending time on the clit, circling it, before he withdrew his tongue and sucked.

"Zen!" Everything was pulsing now, ready to go off like a firework the way he'd built me up and kept me there. This gargoyle, the bastard, slipped his tongue inside and let me feel exactly how long it was. Thick and firm, Zen pushed his tongue inside me, and I could feel the pause at my g-spot. How he could find it in two seconds, something most of my sexual partners missed, was beyond me. But he sure as hell did it, making my eyes roll back. I could feel the stretch, and it was just his tongue. Hungry for his cock, I could imagine why he wanted to try this first, but it didn't stop my imagination from running wild.

The side of my face sank into the bed. My hands were at a loss for something to grab until they felt something rough and hard. I looked up to see Zen's horns, then gently took one. The sounds of approval that rolled through him urged me on as I took his horns in my hands and held on for the ride.

"Zen," I pleaded. "Zen, I'm close."

"Do it," he commanded, slipping his tongue out only long enough to make his demands. "Release your pleasure on my tongue, my stars."

And with that, I was on fire. That clenching sensation was no longer empty as my body locked down on his tongue. Zen's hands pinning my hips in place lit my skin aflame with sensation. I called his name as the climax hit me and continued, taking me on the most intense ride of my life. Zen lapped it up, hungry for whatever he could claim from my orgasm.

As I came down from the high, he was still devouring what he could, and I had to nudge his horns away. "Zen, that's too much. I can't handle it."

"You can," he insisted, and I had to lie there stimulated, sensitive, pulsing, until he felt satisfied with his meal. Because that's exactly what this was for him, a meal.

I was still catching my breath when he finished, licking my clit one last time before he moved from between my thighs to stare down at me, a very different sort of hunger in his eyes.

"You are a delicacy, Henri."

An embarrassed sound escaped me, and I pressed the side of my face into the bed. Zen stroked my hair and adjusted his wings as he moved.

"You came so beautifully, I am eager to see complete release on your face again."

I reached over for a pillow and pulled it over my face, groaning. "Too direct, Zen."

He chuckled. "I can barely hear you through all that." Moving the pillow gently off me, he set it aside and nudged my knees apart.

"Are you serious?" I laughed.

"I would like to see how you stretch for me," he said.

That caught my attention, and while I was still sensitive after such an overpowering orgasm, I was ready to know how close we were to him feeling comfortable trying. I bit the inside of my cheek as I watched. Admittedly, I felt stretched just from his tongue, and I could still feel the ghost of that initial pinching feeling from it.

Zendrax rubbed one giant palm over each thigh, his expression soft and eyes on me when he moved a finger down and inserted it.

"Tell me if it hurts you."

It didn't, but he quickly inserted a second finger and I gasped. He froze.

"Henri?"

"It just surprised me," I assured him. "I'm not hurt, promise."

He considered my words for a moment, then resumed as he slid the fingers gently in and out, letting me grow accustomed to the size. "Do you think you're ready for the third?"

My eyes rounded as they moved from Zen's face down to his hand. "A third?"

His fingers slipped out of me, and he took them into his mouth as he stood. I was going to ask why he was stopping when I saw the shape of his kilt. The bulge underneath wasn't something I'd had to contend with before, and I'd almost forgotten exactly how big it was considering he acquired his kilt right after our first encounter. His hands moved to the buckles that fastened it around him, and I watched those clawed fingers intently.

"I would like to try a third, if you will allow it today. And once you've recovered from that in a night or two, I will be greatly pleased to give you much more." His words did something to me, making me heated again. Not that I was ready yet, because he was right that I was sore, but the thought alone was really revving my engine.

Zen finished with his kilt and pulled it open, and I stared down at the largest cock I'd ever seen. If I thought it was big as a statue, it was nothing compared to his aroused state. My fingers twitched, considering stroking him, if he would allow it. But Zen beat me to it as he took himself in his own hand.

"If I took you unprepared, I would hurt you, my stars. And that I will not allow." I heard his words, registered them with only a slight delay considering the distraction in front of me, but I could not remove my attention from his hand, slowly stroking up and down. It didn't move as fluidly as a human penis under his touch, but I shouldn't have expected it to, considering how firm everything else about him was. Still, it looked like it felt good and I couldn't wait for my turn at it after the orgasm he just gave me.

"Let's try the third," I said, perhaps with a little too much enthusiasm. Zen smirked, one fang hanging out of those beautiful lips as he moved his free hand back down and re-inserted the two fingers.

"Here it comes," he warned, just before adding the third. I held in the sound of surprise that almost burst out of me. Zen was thick, for sure, and with the length of it on top of that . . . This was already a lot to handle, and I understood then why he wanted to prepare this first time.

"Are you alright?" he asked.

"Yeah," I managed. "I just . . . give me a minute."

He kept his hand still for me, but the other continued to move up and down himself and I watched, imagining this feeling inside me, piecing it together with the scene I had before me.

"I'm going to move," he said. He kept it slow, moving in and out as the sensation of more stretching to accommodate him hit me. The blood in my body didn't seem to know whether to rush south or race for my flushed face and neck. The feeling was delicious, with that slight pinch as his fingers filled me. I took it all, but I knew I'd be sore tomorrow. The feeling fell away, leaving me with a satisfying fullness as I sighed, and Zen flashed me a toothy grin.

"Very good, Henri." He removed his hand, and I made a noise of protest. He chuckled, licked his fingers with that tongue of his, and stopped stroking himself.

"Do I get a turn?" I asked, still staring at his erection.

Zen groaned, getting back on his knees for a better height at the side of my bed as he pulled me close to the edge, sitting me up and facing him. "When I find release, my stars, it will only be here."

He had moved his hand without me noticing, and his thumb brushed against my clit, causing me to jump.

"But it's not fair that I got off and you didn't," I argued.

Zen sighed, brushing hair from the side of my face as he brought his eyes level with mine. "I have taken myself in hand more than once since meeting you, and it does not sate my craving to take you on my cock. I will find my release when you are prepared enough for me to well, and truly fuck you, my stars."

There was absolutely no argument to that, even as my traitorous pussy gave me one good throb at his words. Not that I could handle even a little bit of him right now, but damned if I wasn't excited for when the time would come.

"Rest," Zen ordered, leaning down to kiss me on the lips with care. "I will make you something to eat."

That shook me out of it. "You can cook?"

He had already taken a few steps away, tail moving back and forth as he balanced his graceful steps, but the look he threw me over his shoulder was playful. "How do you think I fed myself in my realm? Your ingredients and tools may be unfamiliar, but I have seen enough of the workings of your stove that I would like to try. Will you allow me the use of what I can find in your kitchen?"

Who would have thought the first guy to offer to cook for me wouldn't even be human? I grinned. "Zen, you're an absolute dream, do you know that? It's all yours. Have at it."

He laughed, and I went to sit up in bed when I realized how badly my legs were shaking, my muscles were jelly. Fine, another shower could wait a few minutes while I lay back on the bed and basked in the aftermath.

Finally, that gorgeous gargoyle was mine.

# Chapter Seventeen

## Zendrax

The sun dipped down and released me from its grasp. I had stoned for the day, unable to keep the grin off my face. Last night with Henri was more than I could have imagined. My stars cried out so beautifully as she came apart on my tongue. And the way she took my fingers . . . my cock still remembered the demand it stirred in me to watch her stretching open, preparing herself so that I could take her next time. I brought my fingers to my mouth, hoping to taste whatever remnants of Henri I could, growling in satisfaction as the last traces of her scent still lingered. It would be disappointing when I bathed later, but I could always replenish her delicious scents again.

When I was in complete control of myself, I stood and stretched my wings. Looking down, I noticed the white card placed at my feet.

*The Mistress calls in her boon.*

It was time then. I looked up at Henri's window. We had already agreed that she would rest today. She was going somewhere with her friends and would not be back right at sunset. This would be as good a time as any to address this boon.

Letting gravity pull me down off the side of the building, I tumbled a few wingspans before catching the air around me and gliding back up. It took little time at all to make it to The Crossroads. The path was now so familiar to me, and I knew the best places to stay out of sight from the humans.

Down in the belly of the den of monsters, I found the same collared male that had greeted me upon my first visit to the club.

"Good evening," he greeted, that mischievous smile still on his face as he eyed me up and down. "The Mistress is expecting you, and I'm to take you to her."

I nodded and followed down the hall of sconces to the room in the very back. There was not much activity yet at The Crossroads, but the night was still young, and the monsters were still waking up to play.

At the end of the hall, my guide knocked on the door. "Zendrax, the gargoyle, Mistress." And with his announcement, he left, winking at me as he passed.

"Enter." My attention turned from the demon to the door as the voice of The Mistress commanded my notice. As she bid, I opened the door and moved inside, adjusting my wings through the doorframe as I did so. If the scent wasn't enough to indicate the room's purpose, the scene before me was. The room was dripping with black velvet, a bed, a strange chair of straps and buckles, and a wall with racks and shelves of strange implements. The Mistress sat perched on another such chair, but with none of the buckles fastened. With a leg crossed over the other knee, her head tilted back as she inhaled a strange pipe, slowly letting the smoke blow through her lips. She wore black leather in a stark contrast to her moonglow skin. Those red eyes latched onto my gaze, transfixing me in place.

"I call in my boon, Zendrax the Slicer."

How she knew my battlefield moniker, I wasn't sure, but my claws had the sudden itch to rise to the title. Tearing through my enemies was a point of honor for me, but now it remained one of the last remnants of who I was before the fall of Stoneforge.

"What would you have me do, Mistress?" I couldn't keep the unease from my voice.

She took a long pull from her pipe, letting the smoke blow out slowly as she studied me with a smile. "There's a serpent in the river and it's bothering some of my more lucrative clients."

My brow furrowed as I studied the smoke she blew from her lips. It curled and slithered, imitating a snake in the water.

"Be a dear and go kill it for me." She waved her hand, and the serpent disappeared, the smoke resuming a more natural path through the room.

"And with this task, my debt will be repaid?" I asked.

She nodded, inspecting her pipe. "It will be repaid."

I hesitated. This would be the time to ask about the elusive gargoyle, but I wasn't certain what a being of deals and contracts like The Mistress would make of giving me information without another bargain. Surely this would cost me something extra, unless Stefan found the information I sought and offered it to me freely.

"Whatever is weighing so heavily on your mind, speak it or leave." She took another pull from her pipe, coal red eyes pinning me in place. She would have made a formidable adversary, but I thanked the skies that I wouldn't have to experience it.

"I saw a strange, winged figure the other night. It prowls the skies not far from my rooftops. It appeared to be a gargoyle, from what I could see. Do you know if there are others in this place?" I know what Stefan said, even so, I had to try.

The Mistress blew a long trail of smoke, eyeing me with a mild interest. "I suppose I could make a small deal with you for the information you seek. Once our current deal is complete, that is."

A non-answer, but the opportunity for something more substantial. "Very well, Mistress. I will slay your serpent, and my inquiries will wait until I bring you news of my victory."

She smiled. "Good. I await word of your success."

Her tone left no room for disappointment. And with that, I left The Crossroads.

# Chapter Eighteen

## Henri

Zen could read, right? I mean, I could already tell he was smart, and he was definitely observant. But could he read the note I left taped to the window? Would he be able to read it for the same reasons he could speak our language? I should have thought of that before I took the bus to the park so close to sunset. The last thing I wanted was to disappoint him by being away, but I'd had the powerful urge to come see this place, and I followed it. Either way, I came here for inspiration, not a date with my gargoyle.

My cheeks heated at the idea, though. I knew Zen couldn't risk being seen by regular people, and I was okay with that, but the idea of going out somewhere together was thrilling. This park would be pretty safe this time of night. Hell, just about any park would be, as long as it wasn't too close to a business district or something. A place like Riverview Park had so many trees and so little reason to be out in the middle of the night that it should be safe enough. And I'd seen him stick to the side of buildings in the shadows like it was an art-form. Even The Crossroads could be a fun place to go, if we were ever seeking out the particular *vibe* of a place like that.

Taking a deep breath of the crisp night air, I mounted the last few steps before the platform where my hopes and dreams would someday sit if I won the contest. What a gorgeous place for a statue. Right where my family would have to look at it.

*No, don't bring that pettiness into your art.* But I didn't bother trying to keep the grin off my face at the thought, either.

*Focus, Henri.*

Standing in front of the empty platform, I could almost taste how badly I wanted to win. The blank slate waited, welcoming a sculpture to adorn it, but I was still at a loss as to what would win the judges' votes. With a sigh through my nose, I moved back a few paces to the nearest bench and sat. One foot across the opposite knee, and the other foot tapping out my frustration.

"What in the world do I put there?" I asked. "What says 'Riverview Park' enough to win the—"

Standing fast enough to spin my vision, I sprinted to the other side of the empty platform. Down the walking paths, dodging curated rose bushes and trimmed hedges, I pushed towards the fenced off viewing deck. Past the wrought iron fencing and a brass plate declaring the founding of the park, I looked over the edge into the river itself. Wide, with thick currents and several yards down from where I stood, flowed the deceptively calm river. I knew there were supposed to be strong currents underneath, and it was big enough for commercial boats to pass through the city under the tall bridges that connected the north and south halves of the town.

The river itself. What else was more central to the founding of Crossgate? *How's that for an organic shape, Simon?* And I could frame it, quite literally, in a gothic window. What got stuck at the front of my mind was a display of nature trails I'd seen in a wildlife park once. A sculpted model showing off the gothic shapes I love as a window frame for the river. The space between the river shape and the frame could be completely empty, a hole through which you can see the town hall on the opposite side of the river.

I looked up at the building in question. Yeah, no matter what time of year, if I have the sculpture positioned correctly, it will frame that building, too. My heart was hammering so hard I wondered if I should be concerned. I pulled out my phone and began to take notes on my ideas before they slipped away from me. I went back to the platform, back to the benches and sat down as I kept looking up to the view, then back down for more notes.

No telling how long I was there, typing up every thought that crossed my mind, when a soft brush of air from behind caused me to shiver and look over my shoulder. I wasn't ready for how close Zendrax was, and I jumped as his hand landed on my shoulder from behind the bench.

"There you are," he mused. "Have I mentioned how much I enjoy the look on your face when you're focused?"

I stuck my tongue out at him, which only earned me a soft chuckle as he moved to crouch in front of the bench, placing a hand on each of my knees. "How are you feeling tonight?"

I caught my bottom lip in my teeth as my eyes shot south. I knew exactly what was under that kilt, and I hadn't been quiet about wanting it. "I feel fine," I said. "Just like I said yesterday."

The growl from his throat was nearly inaudible, but I caught the whisper of it as his eyes lit with hunger. "You keep tempting me, Henri."

I snorted. "Did you think I haven't been trying to?"

He moved up with a warrior's grace, that tongue stretching out to lick the shell of my ear as he murmured, "Patience. You will have everything I can give you soon enough."

The shiver that ran through me left me without breath for a second, while one clawed hand moved from my knee to stroke the side of my face.

"Now?" I asked.

"Soon," he promised. "First, I have a task from The Mistress."

"Oh," I answered, more somber now. "She turned in her favor?"

"She did," Zen confirmed, and stood with a sigh. "I would like to complete it tonight, or at least get a start on it. The task laid out will not be easy, and it weighs heavy on me that I owe a boon that has yet to be repaid to such a creature as her."

"I understand." Disappointing, sure, but a good reason to wait. When I took Zendrax's dick, I wanted his focus wholly on me. Because if he could do all that with just his tongue, what was in store when he gave me the rest? "Can I help with the favor?"

"No, I'm afraid it's something I must do alone. The Mistress sends me after a creature causing trouble at the bottom of the river."

"No way, in the river? There's nothing down there bigger than a catfish. We'd know about something dangerous down there." The longer I spoke, the less convinced I was. After all, I had no idea what things lurked in this city just a few months ago. If The Mistress and her magic could keep humans from knowing about these creatures, who's to say there's not a monster in the river too?

"Nothing more than a fish, my stars, nothing to fret over. While I would not put you in danger, I'm certain it's nothing I can't handle. I've killed a boxogra larger than this river is wide, so whatever lurks below, I can take care of it."

"What's a boxog—wait, no, I actually don't think I want to know," I said. My phone alarm went off, and I looked down at the screen, reminding me that the last bus would come soon. "Crap, I'm out of time."

"What is it?" Zen asked.

"I came here to get inspiration for my big sculpture project," my voice raised as I remembered what I came up with. "And I figured it out! I figured out what I want to make."

Throwing my arms around his neck, he lifted me to his full height in his arms. I was startled at first, but it was so easy to snuggle in, despite the coolness of his skin in the already cool night air.

"Wonderful news," he purred, peppering my neck with kisses. "I can't wait to see it."

"Wait," I looked over his shoulder to the viewing deck, "can you help me with one more thing before I catch the bus?"

"What is it, my stars?" he asked, and my stomach did a flip at the pet name.

"Can you take me up, but just a few feet? I want to take some pictures of the shape of the river."

Zen pulled back, looking me in the eye. "Are you certain?"

My heart was pounding, and my hands became clammy at my own suggestion. "No, but I need them. And I'm not sure your claws will be able to operate a smart phone."

He looked down at the phone in my hands, nodding. "I will hold on tightly. You do not have to fear when you're with me."

Despite the reaction my body was having at the idea of leaving the ground, I smiled. "I know. Thank you."

He walked us over to where the fence stood, the last barrier between the park and the plummet to the river below. With a death grip on my phone, the record button already pressed so I could pull images from the video later, I wrapped my other arm tightly around his neck, practically strangling Zen as he leapt off the edge.

An ugly squeal left my throat as his wings snapped open and he glided over the river. I barely managed to point my phone in the right direction, capturing the moonlit water in all its curves and ripples. Somewhere between ten seconds and an hour later—or at least that's what it felt like—I was already begging for solid ground.

"Enough, down, please, now." I whimpered as we turned mid-air, a few flaps lifting us high enough to glide back to the platform where we started. I stopped recording and clutched my phone to my chest as I held my breath the rest of the way. When I finally felt Zen touch down, I opened my eyes and melted in his arms.

"Are you well?" he asked, concern written on his face as he inspected every part of me.

"I'm fine, now that we're done." He reluctantly let me wiggle out of his arms and onto the sidewalk, where I was able to calm down. "Thank you for your help. I'm sorry, it looks like my fear of heights is still there."

"No apologies." He placed his palm against my cheek, and I leaned into it. "Was your image capturing a success?"

"Let me see." I pulled out my phone and reviewed what I got. "Yeah, this looks amazing. More details than I'd get if I just looked online, I think. Most pictures aren't going to be from directly above."

Zen nodded, then moved his head sharply as he looked past me and through the park. "Your transportation draws close."

"Shoot!" I darted away down the sidewalk. "Come see me before you do your boon thingy?"

"As you wish it, it will be done," he answered. "The task can wait a short while if it is for you."

My face heated and a grin spread across my cheeks. As I sprinted for the last bus of the night, I left behind Zen's warm chuckle and the flap of wings.

# Chapter
# Nineteen

## Zendrax

Henri returned home not long after I had arrived from the river and joyously described her artistic ideas in great detail while I warmed by the fire and listened in content bliss. I would attend to my boon tonight, but first I would I spend some time much in the same way I would spend it before battle back in Stoneforge, with my stars none the wiser. This was better, yes. This time was for reflecting and enjoying the people around me before taking on a dangerous task, and right now, that meant Henri.

We didn't speak of the boon, and I hoped to have made light enough of the effort that she wouldn't worry for me, but the truth remained that no battle was a certainty and a wise warrior would not treat it as such. The setting may be new, and the pizza was certainly a different matter from taking meal with my clan, but all the same, I took in what I cared about in preparation for battle. Henri's smile, her laughter, the softness of her hands. As my mother would often tell me, your heart is the source of your warrior's spirit.

I left Henri because she was trying not to fall asleep, unfolding her grand plans for her sculpture, my heart light at her happiness and the inspiration that had her in its grasp. But my time with Henri had to come to an end as she began to yawn. I had to say goodbye as she moved toward her bed, and I shifted my focus to the task at hand.

Leaving her window, I made my way to one of the rooftops a few blocks away, where I could overlook the river. The moon cast her light on the surface of the water as it danced downstream. What creature lurked beneath? I hadn't enough clues, but there was only one way to know. Stretching my wings, I looked for any eyes, any lit windows facing this part of the river. The blessing of this "old town," as Henri called it, was the neglected walls by the riverside. Debris, a dumpster, and an abandoned vehicle were all that remained to see from the side of this building, and so I tipped my weight over the edge of the rooftop and sped to the edge of the water.

Wading above my knees, the ends of my wings dipped into the water as I scanned the murky depths for movement. The river was wide and deep, giving me suspicion of underwater caves in the limestone. It would be easy for a beast to hide within, coming out only to hunt. I shed my kilt on the banks of the river and moved deeper up to my waist. The current was strong, a pull that would carry a human away. But the stone of a gargoyle could contend with the water, and so could my breath. I needed very little air, unless I wished to speak, and so I filled my lungs, then plunged down.

The water was somewhat clearer where the current carried the mud and moss downstream, leaving views to the depths. The bottom of the river was mostly still, but the edges held dark shadows, confirming my suspicion of caves.

I pushed to the surface to take another breath, moving through the water against the current while searching beneath the surface for a sign. My weight worked against me, but my wings helped displace much of the water to move me forward. Finally, I saw movement.

Deep, deep where the shadows climbed toward the surface of the rushing water, something in the riverbed was kicking up ominous clouds. My instincts told me something was down there, and it didn't like me intruding on its territory. I surfaced for another deep breath, staring up at the lone moon and giving a thought to Henri before diving to the depths.

I used my wings in an awkward motion to propel me through the water faster. Nothing I hadn't practiced in Stoneforge in the event that I were to fall into the lake at the bottom of the gorge when flying over it, but I hadn't needed to do it since I was a fledgling and my back strained with the unused motions as I pressed on. A large, dark shadow slithered in and out of a pit in the riverbed's wall. So deep was this place that it surprised me that the cliffs were not higher from the wearing down of the water, but there were many mysteries surrounding Crossgate, and I would have to leave them for another day. All I needed to know right now was that my suspected target was within those alcoves.

Reaching the bottom, I flared my wings, if only to steady myself in the current as I let my weight sink me into the sand. Stepping carefully, I approached the cavernous entrance, peering into the maw of shadows.

The water was nearly still, and I couldn't see a thing. Not wanting to rely only on my sight, I spread my wings wider to feel any change in the current around me and focused on what I could hear despite the rushing water.

The beast found me before I found it. I was knocked sideways as a huge, scaled body swept at my back. I dragged what I could of my tail and one clawed foot across it as I righted myself and it swam away. Once I was on my feet again and facing the beast, I got my first look at it. With silver and sand-colored scales to fit the riverbed, it was more serpent than fish. I could spread my hand open and still not completely cover one of its eyes. With a shape perhaps a bit like an eel and the head and fangs of a snake, the thing struck again.

This time, I could move to the side and take less of a hit, but the beast was quick. And yet, not quick enough to avoid my claws as I dug both hands against its side, sinking my fingers into the flesh of the beast. The beast shook with fury, tail writhing as it slipped from my clawed grasp and swam back to face me again.

With another lunge, the serpent made to strike with its fangs. I avoided it, but so too did the beast evade my counterattack as it slipped into the cave swift as a storm. I would have snarled if I was above water, but the air I held would only last a few more minutes. I couldn't let the beast trap me in its cave without a fresh breath.

Moving up to the surface took all my strength, my weight trying to sink to the riverbed. But I moved upward for another breath before trying the cave. I was halfway to the surface when I felt the current surge. Looking down just too late, the beast bit into my leg and dragged me down. Thrashing, it shook as it hauled me into the cave. I twisted my body, moving to sink claws into the face of my captor. It had carried me so far down, so swiftly, that by the time I could assault it, the creature had already released me from its jaws as it poised for another, more consuming bite.

Flaring my wings out, I moved just far enough to the side to avoid being swallowed. My eyes darted to the surface outside the cave. I would need air soon, but if this beast would not let me have it, then I would have to deal with it quickly.

As the serpent slithered past me in its failed strike, I latched onto the tail and began pulling myself up its body, one clawed hand at a time. Pricks of blood flowed off its back from where I dug my claws and climbed, the body beginning to thrash as I drew close to the head. I was nearly there when the beast slammed into a cave wall, causing me to nearly slip as I took the hit to my side, but I held true.

I finally reached the head, the beast thoroughly enraged as it twisted and curled through the underwater cave. It was still so dark that I could barely see as the beast neared the mouth of what must be its den, but I could feel everything I needed to feel as I roared and sank my claws into one of the eyes.

The serpent jolted, but I dug deeper, ripping through the layers and blinding the beast. My other hand held tight to the side, feeling for the gills where I raked claws just inside the tender organ. The thrashing became sporadic, electric, jolting as I tore through flesh and scale. Then, the beast tried to slam us against the wall once more, but I held fast as I ripped through it.

The water, already so dark, was now clouded with blood and worse from the beast that seemed to know it was losing the battle. I bowed my head briefly, the only acknowledgement I could give my foe while underwater, and with one last effort, I plunged my claws into the soft underbelly beneath its jaw and ended the serpent for good.

The need to catch my breath meant I had no time to dwell on the creature I had slain. Mouth open, it was easy to choose a trophy of proof for The Mistress as I freed a fang from its maw, then swam. Everything strained, and as the fervor of battle wore off, the sting where the beast's teeth pierced my leg to drag me down began to burn. I would be sore in the places that collided into the limestone walls, but I had emerged the victor and a night of rest would recover me well.

When I broke the surface, I swallowed up the air with greed. Pulling myself downstream, I found the secluded place where I had entered the water and climbed onto the rocky bank where I could roll onto my back and allow my body to stop moving.

Staring at the fang, nearly the length of my arm, it was a wonder this creature had even been allowed to reach this size in this city of monsters. I knew there were plenty of things in this place that could have defeated the serpent, but likely enough, I was the best candidate that owed The Mistress a boon. Letting the fang fall from my hand as I closed my eyes and focused on breathing, I waited for my body to dry off, the aching to ease.

With this task done, I could stop worrying about my boon to The Mistress and focus on protecting my rooftops, on protecting Henri. With a groan, more eager to finish my task than to let my body fully rest, I made my way into the shadowed alleys that would take me to Old Town unseen. Tucking the tooth into the side of my garment, I made my way home.

The city overflowed with sounds and lights, something I had grown used to. And perhaps it was the adrenaline from the fight with the serpent that still burned in me, but I remained on alert as I moved from one brick-clad building to another, climbing slowly between windows and taking advantage of nooks in the architecture. The sensation of being watched struck me, and I whirled around to face the empty alley. Nothing moved, still as the night, but still my eyes caught at the roofline where a smooth expanse of stone capped the corner—save for three streaked marks gouged into it.

Snarling, I leapt from my wall to scale the opposite one, rushing to the surface of the alley where the light of the city would allow me to inspect it. I did not know enough of this realm to know what else could have made such marks in the stone. But my heart told me it was the lunging escape of a clawed being with wings. I whipped my head up and around, searching for the shape of a gargoyle—or something like it—but found nothing.

Finally, looking to the skies, the few stars twinkled out as the threat of morning approached. An ill omen, something that did not set right with me. If it were truly one of my kind, why hide? And if it were not, what manner of monster disturbed my senses as it prowled around my rooftops?

With a growl at the encroaching sun, I slipped away to the rooftop where I could spy Henri's window, safely closed and undisturbed. A sigh of relief with my last breath as the sun burst over the skyline and imprisoned my form for another cycle.

# Chapter Twenty

## Henri

Humming along with my music as I sketched with fervor, I sat in the middle of the room surrounded by poster boards, sketch books, measuring tape, and printed out pictures of the river. At least it kept me occupied since Zen left last night. Which was ridiculous, of course, because by now he had done whatever he was going to do and was on a rooftop somewhere turned to stone. I'm sure most of the action happened while I was asleep, so the outcome of the fight had already been determined, but I still worried. Sleeping until noon, followed by a bowl of cereal and anxiety over this boon thing he was doing, made me search for distraction. Thankfully, I had the perfect thing for that as I looked over the chunk of stone that I planned to turn into my sculpture. It would be a tight timeline, but I was ready for the challenge now that I knew what I wanted to make.

A giant gothic window frame where I could showcase the bumps and curves of a river that overflowed it. A bird's-eye view of one of the most iconic parts of the founding of Crossgate City, and it was a perfect model for the contest.

"Yes!" I was giddy as I capped my marker, finishing the plans for the frame itself to reference later. When my alarm went off, interrupting my music, my attention snapped to the window where the first beams of sunset blossomed across the skyline, and I nibbled at my bottom lip. Rain pattered against the huge windows all evening, adding a soothing background to my work. Now, the end of the rain showers drizzled down the panes in minute rivers, catching the droplets and pooling them together until they reached the bottom ledge and fell away in the golden sunset.

Standing and swearing at my foot that had fallen asleep, I cleaned up. I organized the project supplies, tucking them near the base of the stone and draping the sheet over it. A quick dusting and sweeping took care of the rest of the apartment, then I could pull the sheets off the bed and other furniture. By the time I finished, I looked out to a darkening sky, and my heart sped up. Zen could be here any time now, provided he was done with that other task he had.

Clearing my throat, I made my way to the bathroom. "You're not cleaning up for a gargoyle, Henri. Boss bitches don't revolve their whole evening around some guy. It's just time to take a break, that's all."

Taking the world's quickest shower, I threw on a big t-shirt and found a seat at the table where I pulled my favorite takeout menus from the nearby drawer. Checking to make sure I had a pair of pants on the coat rack, I turned my attention to dinner plans. Zen may have seen me in the no-pants club plenty of times, but that didn't mean I was going to walk down and grab delivery like that.

A rattle at the window had me beaming as I looked up to meet Zen's gaze.

"You came," I said as he stepped through the window, closing it behind him. Drinking him in, I eyed the kilt and let my imagination run wild. The curve of his shoulders, the sway of his tail, the tips of his wings that still dripped from the rain we'd gotten. But there, on his leg, was a strange patch of rock that hadn't looked like that before.

Frowning, I gestured to it. "What happened to your leg?"

"I am fine. Are you well? Has anything happened while I sunned?" Zendrax asked.

Taking another step closer, I couldn't pull my eyes from his leg. "Nothing, just a normal day. Zen, what happened?"

He sighed, "It was pierced by the beast from the river, but as I sunned, I healed. Such is true of any injury, as long as a part of me has not broken off completely."

Panic and bile shot up my throat. "Sit! Get in here, are you alright? Do you need medicine? Can gargoyles even use medicine? Oh my God, what do we do? Do I need to call someone? Stefan?"

"Henri! Henri I am truly alright." His attempts to placate me were only doing so much, but it helped that I could see him walk on his own without much trouble. As he spoke, his hand raised in gesture and I spotted the white stick he carried.

"What's that?" I asked.

My gargoyle stepped closer, setting the stick by the fireplace. "The tooth of the beast I will bring back to The Mistress."

I balked. "That's a *tooth*? Oh my god, are you okay? Is that what punctured you? You fought something like that?" My limbs went numb. "Something like that was in the *river*?"

"It is no more, and I am well," Zen said, stepping toward me. "Do not focus on the trophy. I will have all of your attention tonight."

That drew my focus from the terrifying tooth to a set of hungry jade eyes. My pulse quickened in my neck as I stood from the chair with a shy smile. "You have it."

In two more steps, Zen was able to wrap an arm around my back and press his mouth to mine as we met in an impassioned kiss. I grinned against his mouth and met him with the same fervor. He pulled back, and I caught my breath.

"Are you truly well? You have seen the other creatures that prowl this realm. None have disturbed you in my absence?"

"No, is everything okay?" I asked. "Something has you rattled."

Zen paused, shaking his head slowly. "I worry for you, my stars. I do not like not knowing what lurks here."

Sweet as cotton fucking candy.

*I literally cannot keep waiting.*

Pulling myself up with my arms around his neck, I stole another kiss, which he met and deepened. Coming up for breath, I pulled back enough to get a good look at his face. "I feel completely better," I said hopefully. "If you want to go all the way."

The growl from his throat sent a delightful chill down my back. The claws on the hand he'd wrapped around my back dug into my skin ever so slightly and my awareness sharpened on them. "It would be my honor."

I didn't have time to be excited over his answer before a pair of hands grabbed the back of my thighs and pulled me off my feet, up against his body. Flinging my arms around his neck to hold on, Zen nipped at my ear and rumbled into the side of my neck, "The taste of you has haunted me since I first ran my tongue across your skin and into your depths, and I will have it again. Now."

Zen carried me to the bed, laying me down and dragging me to the edge, where he spread my legs apart. One ankle jolted in surprise as his thin tail wound around it to hold my leg in place, his hands pressing into the thickest part of my thighs as he unveiled what he wanted. Leaning over me, he inhaled as his wings flexed behind him, reminiscent of curling toes or a gasping breath. I gripped the bedding beneath me as he planted a kiss dangerously high on one thigh, then the other.

Wet heat flooded me at the ferocity in Zen's eyes, the raw display of hunger. I yelped as he pulled off my panties in one fluid motion, and then all I had left was my shirt. Eagerly, I helped him get it off of me and his hands immediately found the skin at my sides, claws lightly pressing down in thin lines as he moved to palm my hips. He moved his gaze up my stomach, pausing briefly at my breasts, and then landing on my flushed face with a grin. The most wicked expression I've seen from Zen before pinned me in place.

"You lay a feast before me, my stars. Do not be surprised when I see fit to have my fill."

"Oh," I barely whispered out, when my breath escaped my lungs with the movement of Zen pulling me close until his tongue was inside me and I made a sound of surprise. My hands flew down to grab onto anything, and my fingers wrapped around his horns, earning me a pleased rumble from Zen as he feasted. Because that's what this was for him, a feast. He truly meant what he said.

In the fog of it all, Zen's rain-chilled claws scraped against my flushed skin in a thrilling contrast of temperatures. For every part of me that raged in heat, there was a cool stone muscle to meet it. A thousand nerve endings screamed at the contrast. Cold, heat, skin, stone, all tearing through the thin line between pain and pleasure.

"Zen." The only warning I could give either of us before one fang rubbed at the side of my clit as his tongue thrust one last time before my climax. With all of my remaining strength, I held on for dear life as Zendrax continued his assault on my senses, forcing me to last longer than I could ever remember going before, as muscles clenched and flooded.

"More," he demanded, barely slipping his tongue out long enough to form the command before resuming his efforts. But I was on fire, parts of me still screaming, begging for pause or for more, I wasn't certain.

"Every time I secure a taste of you, my cravings deepen me to madness," Zen soothed in my ear as he pulled me close enough for our hips to meet. Leaning over me, one rough hand brushed the hair from my face. Damp, either from the shower I'd had just before he arrived, or from the sweat he pulled from me with the strain of what we'd been doing. My arms found his neck as I pulled him down to meet me in a kiss, tasting myself on his lips in the process.

"My stars," he groaned, pressing one last firm kiss before a hand at my thigh distracted me. "Look at me, Henri. Are you truly ready?"

My gaze flicked back to his, and I nodded with fervor. Every nerve in my body was overloaded. From the scrape of my nipples against his rough chest, the prick of his claws as he grasped my hip with tenderness to avoid breaking skin, but also the firm hand to keep me in place. An emptiness my body craved to be filled. I felt him move a knee to the bed, holding himself over me with both arms.

"Please." The whisper barely left me when I gasped at the solid feeling at my entrance.

Zen pushed into me, no more than an inch, as the burn of being stretched hit me. The corner of my eyes watered, and he stopped.

"Henri-"

"Don't stop," I begged. "Just take it slow. I want to feel all of you."

Zen leaned down to kiss me tenderly, at the same time he slid in a little more. The burn was present, but it faded quickly enough as he pulled blood to other sensitive parts of my body. Kissing my neck, claws scraping against the round of my ass.

"One of these days, my stars, I will spend the night kissing every star on your body until I lose count and have to begin again," he murmured as he filled me until I felt like there was no room for more.

"I don't think we'd make it that far," I teased, my breath shallow and hot. Nudging him gently until he lifted enough that I could try to see around my stomach to where we connected, but I could tell he wasn't all the way inside. My eyes rounded. "There's more of you."

He chuckled, kissing my neck, then urging me to lie back down. "I assure you, I have plans to show you more another time. Right now, let me enjoy this without hurting you. You've come to mean so much to me, my stars."

As his words sank into my heart and carved a place to stay, Zen pulled partially out of me before sliding back in. My eyes might as well have rolled to the back of my head, I was dizzy with sensation. It was so much, and so good, I had to do something with my hands. One arm wrapped nicely over Zen's shoulder, and the other reached as far around to his back as I could, scraping my blunt nails against him.

A rumbly moan eased from him as his face sank to my neck, kissing my flushed skin. The pace picked up, and I clung tighter as we moved together, the bedframe creaking with every thrust.

"Fuck, Zen," I hissed as he wound me tighter and tighter.

"Such a tight little thing you are, Henri, and wet as the banks of Stoneforge Lake. A siren trying to pull me in and drown me." Zen nipped my ear and gave one hard push at the same time, toppling me. I gasped, holding on for the climax that struck me like lightning. Zen kept going, careful not to thrust any deeper than he had been, and I barely had the mind to marvel at his restraint when I knew very well there was more of him to be had. When he stilled for a heartbeat, my walls still clenching around him, he offered a guttural sound to my ceiling. Not a roar, but something just as primal. His wings snapped open, flexed as far as they could go in the space my apartment offered. I felt him spill himself inside, and the two of us rode out the rest of our ecstasy until I was a panting mess and Zen was planting careful kisses across my cheeks and shoulders. It was easy to bask in Zen's affections, my own hands reaching up to stroke the side of his face with the same tenderness he showed me.

"Worth the wait," I said, finally breaking the quiet that had settled over us.

A warm rumble from Zen's chest showed his amusement as he rolled us on the bed, so that I could lie next to him as he pulled out of me. The sensation of being filled did not leave with his cock, and the texture of his cum was so much thicker than a human's that it wasn't making a lot of progress seeping out of me as I moved. A small experimental wiggle made me think I could get the excess out, but I didn't have to worry about as much mess as I thought I'd have to, considering the quantity.

"How are you feeling?" Zen asked, running a hand down my arm.

"Fucking amazing." I grinned.

He raised one eyebrow. "No soreness?"

"Maybe a little," I admitted, tucking myself under his chin as he wrapped an arm and a wing around me. "Still worth it. If you want to go a little rougher next time, I'm very interested in seeing if the rest of you can fit. I think I like it a little rough."

He chuckled, and I could feel his tail sneaking its way up my calf to join in on the cuddling. "Do you now? I have no plans on pushing you further today, my stars, but I look forward to watching your tight little body swallow all of me."

*This gargoyle.* Was it the cultural barrier that let him say these things? Was everyone from his world like this in bed? Or did Zen talk like this just because he was Zen? If I didn't agree with him about not risking another round tonight, I'd already be on top of him right—

*Creak.*

I moved to sit up, and Zen moved his arm and wing to make room. "What was that?" The words barely left my mouth when the creak sounded again, and the whole bed shifted as the frame snapped free of the footboard, sending the mattress slanting on the floor. The headboard followed in much the same way, leaving us planted flat on the ground.

In shock, I stared at the headboard which Zen prevented from falling on us, and then the floor, which was now a foot closer to my sleeping arrangements than it had been a minute ago.

"Henri, are you alright?" Zen asked.

But the only sound I could make was the laugh that bubbled up and out of me. I just fucked a gargoyle, probably a thousand pounds of stone, give-or-take. If anything, it was a miracle we hadn't broken it in the middle of our passion.

"Henri?"

I rubbed the tears of laughter from my eyes with the heel of my hand and nuzzled into Zen's side. "It's fine, but I'm going to have to commission a very specifically sturdy bedframe from Chloe. Let's just hope she doesn't ask too many questions."

# Chapter Twenty-One

## Zendrax

"Henri," I murmured to the sleeping form on the mattress. I brushed a bit of her sunset curls aside so I could see her face. Groaning, she pulled the blankets tighter around herself and I chuckled. "Henri, I must go."

She was awake now, blinking up at me through the haze of sleep. We had pulled the mattress away from the broken frame and spent the rest of the night hours together. The pizza boxes were still on the floor nearby, and her electronic device was still softly playing music. But after the full night we'd had, it was no wonder Henri had drifted off to sleep.

"No, sorry, I'm up," she said, trying to prop herself upright.

"Stay, sleep," I insisted, gently pushing her back down onto the mattress. "I must take the prize to The Mistress, and daylight will be here soon enough. I only wanted to make sure you knew."

A sound of great exasperation escaped her as I let her pull me down for a kiss.

"You're really warm," she mumbled.

"As you slept, I spent some time by the fireplace," I explained. "Is it too much for you?"

Henri's smile turned sheepish as she pulled the blankets around to hide some of her face. "It almost hurts, but it doesn't. It makes me wonder what temperature play feels like."

My brows dipped as I mulled over the term. "To play with temperatures?"

She rolled her face into the blankets, muffling her laughter. "To play with temperatures during sex," she explained.

A rumble in my chest caught her attention as I leaned down for one more kiss. "Temptress," I mused. "I must go, but I will be back to find out more about this temperature play when the sun releases me from her starless prison. I am eager to see what faces you'll make."

She buried more of herself in the blankets as I pulled away. "How can you say this stuff with a straight face?"

I chuckled as I made my way to the window. "I'll be back for you, Henri."

"See you tonight," she called, and as I closed the window behind me, it appeared she was already asleep once more.

A cloud of smoke perfumed the hallway as Stefan opened the door to the office where The Mistress waited. She was lounging with her head laid back as her snow-white hair draped down the sofa, a pipe in her hand.

"You can go, Stefan," she said, her ruby eyes not moving from the ceiling until we heard the door close as he left. When we were alone, she moved her head just enough that she could pierce me with her fiery stare. "Well?"

I took two steps forward, setting the tooth on the table before her. The corners of her mouth moved upward ever so slightly.

"It is done," I said. "Now, may I know of the gargoyle in the city?"

"Another deal was struck, just a week ago. I am not the one who made the deal. Another portal demon did it, and I will deal with those encroaching on *my* city." The Mistress moved the pipe to her lips, taking a long, slow draw from it before blowing the smoke out in a lazy ribbon. "But this gargoyle remains under my domain as long as they remain within my borders. They are under the same rules as you, to remain out of sight of the humans." Her head laid back again. "Unlike you, they haven't been sighted."

My wings tensed, contracting to me. So, the instincts clawing at my mind have been correct. The thought sat poorly with me, and I wouldn't be able to rest without knowing what our dynamic would be within this city. Gargoyles, at least from my realm, could be very territorial. "Where can I find them?"

The black clawed tips of her fingers tapped on her pipe in thought while she watched me. "I'm sure you'll run into each other, eventually. Not many things can take to the skies, even in Crossgate City."

"You don't know where they are, then?" I asked.

She shrugged, paying more attention to the swirling smoke from her pipe than to me. "Old Town, close to the river, perhaps."

Clenching my jaw, I remained still. Losing my temper in front of her would earn me no favors. "Thank you, Mistress."

Her eyes, which had been so casual in their wanderings, snapped to me as she smiled. "Polite. Wise. One more piece of advice, Zendrax, the gargoyle you seek is from your very same realm. Be cautious of that. You are dismissed."

My mind raced, even as my body was able to calmly walk out of the office and down the hall. What could she have meant by that?

# Chapter Twenty-Two

## Henri

Highly inappropriate activities filled my dreams.

Highly inappropriate, involving wet stone and the rooftop of my building. Waking hours Henri would be appalled. And maybe a little bit terrified of the heights.

I woke up several hours later to bright sunlight; the rays glaring through the window onto the mattress. I pressed my face into the sheets, disoriented at first because I wasn't exactly in the corner of the room I was used to waking up in. I lay there, considering the splintered mess that once was the bedframe. Still, I managed to get up, clean up, make myself a smoothie, and get to work. After all, the more I got done during the day, the more freedom I had with my gargoyle when the sun went down.

I kept a smile on my face with the anticipation of his nighttime visit while I finished my plans and started on the stone itself. Music blasted over the sounds of my work on the stone, and the hours slipped away. Eventually my stomach pulled me away to make a sandwich, and by the time I saw the tinge of orange outside, I gladly rushed through a shower and cleaned up my apartment.

Pulling a box of peppermint tea from the cabinet, I heard the first scratching at the window. I grinned while setting the box on the counter, then ran for the windowpane. With the night sky outside and my apartment lit up, Zen's shadow was hard to see at first until I pulled the frame open. "Zen!"

My face fell.

Another gargoyle, just as alive and able to move around as Zendrax, only this one didn't look friendly.

"What do you want?" My voice cracked as I took a step back. The new gargoyle's face twisted as it sniffed at the air in my apartment, stepping inside.

"You consort with a shameful, banished failure, human."

My expression snapped to a scowl. "Zen is not shameful!" I backed up, knocking over my stool and grabbing a chisel, holding it between me and the intruder. He laughed, a sound like thunder and bad omens.

The gargoyle sneered. "Zendrax is all that stands between me and a place over Stoneforge that should rightfully be mine. You, human, appear to be the only thing he has taken a liking to in this realm, and you will help me lure him out into the open."

"The hell I will!" Lunging, I knocked the chisel across the thing's chest as it screeched, a long gouge biting into the surface of its rocklike hide.

A stone hand smacked the makeshift weapon from my hand, sending it clattering on the floor behind me. I screamed as he grabbed me, pulling me to his chest and backing out the window as my chisel clattered to the floor.

"No!" I screamed before my throat tightened and my heart skipped. No! Anything but that! The gargoyle had me in his grasp, far too strong for me to get away. He forced me into a position that had me looking at the drop to the streets below, my stomach doing flips the entire time.

"Let go!" I begged, pushing and pulling at the unmoving arm around my rib cage. Panic set in as the gargoyle tipped backwards and we both dropped over the edge. Cold night air pierced through my old t-shirt, and my bare legs had nothing between them and the chill. Up here, so far from the ground, there was little to buffer the wind.

Wind and terror took my voice away, as all I could do was hang on and pray this thing didn't drop me. I found myself clinging to the strange gargoyle's neck in fear. Too high. We were way too high up, and I was going to pass out. Soon. The wind howled in my ears and my body jerked as the strange gargoyle spread his wings and caught the draft, changing course rapidly as he sped out of Old Town.

"Zen!" I screamed, knowing the chances he was near enough to hear me, let alone get to me, were slim. The wind ate up any volume I tried to project as he carried me away. Over the busy streets of Old Town, past the riverside businesses that were mostly asleep for the night, a cloudy night hiding most of the moonlit sky was concealing us from the unknowing city below.

"Where are we going?" I demanded.

The stranger kept his eyes ahead, giving no answer to my question. Finally, after an agonizing flight, we were in the newer business district of Crossgate, where skyscrapers gathered in bundled up blocks. We swooped to the tallest one, a building with a small, flat rooftop platform and one small overhang above a maintenance door. He dropped me unceremoniously onto the rough roof, where I scraped my palms as I tried to catch myself. But I didn't care, because, in that moment, I was on solid ground. The gargoyle strode to the door, tried to pull it open, then grinned.

"You will remain here, human," he ordered, then opened his wings with a snap and flew away.

## Zendrax

I pushed my body harder than I had in a long time in my rush to reach Henri's apartment. A darkened sky was on my side, as the care I usually took to conceal myself was no longer my priority. The first drops of rain began to hit the buildings as I landed on Henri's rooftop. Eating up the distance to the ledge in front of her window, I came to a jarred halt. Gouges slashed into the stone around her window and dug into the ledge beneath my feet.

I nearly ripped the window from its hinges as I entered the apartment. My heart stilled as I took in the fallen seat where Henri was supposed to be working on her art. I stepped forward and bumped into something that rolled across the floor. Crouching down, I picked up one of Henri's precious tools. Gripping it with a snarl, I placed it on her table where it belonged.

Three harsh knocks pounded on her door, and my head snapped up to see whatever intruder I was about to tear to pieces.

"Open up, Henri!" a feminine voice called. "It's Chloe and Simon."

"We brought Pad Thai," called a rougher voice.

Standing to my full height, claws at the ready as my tail swished in anger, I allowed the rattling at the doorknob to continue while I decided what to do with these humans. The door finally swung open to reveal them, and two pairs of wide eyes gawked at me. The woman held a keychain in one hand and the doorknob in the other. A man carrying a large paper bag that smelled of food dropped it.

I knew who they were. These were the ones my stars had claimed when her kin had failed her. I recognized them as the humans in the picture beside Henri's bed.

"She wasn't making it up," Chloe said, barely audible.

"Where is Henri?" Simon demanded.

At my full height, I took the scant few steps where I could stand face to face with them, and they both flinched as I leaned over them, Simon positioning himself slightly in front of Chloe. "That's what I want to know. My stars has been taken."

Chloe pulled out her phone, pressing the illuminated screen even as she kept an eye on me. "I'm calling the police."

"Don't," I said at the same time as Simon. We looked at each other briefly, and he stood to his full height, still much shorter than mine and with a pounding heartbeat.

"You called her something," he said.

"My stars," I affirmed.

"Simon," Chloe whispered, tugging at his sleeve. "We don't know anything about this . . ."

Simon reached over without looking to take her hand. He nodded into the room. "Yeah, we do."

I turned to see what he was gesturing at, even as he took the steps into the apartment. Simon picked up an open sketching book from the table, revealing a page filled with my likeness from several angles.

"Oh," Chloe breathed.

Simon turned to me with the open page. "You guys care about each other, don't you?"

I nodded, pleased to affirm our affection to Henri's friends but frustrated by her absence. She could be in danger. There was no time for this.

"I must go find her," I reaffirmed. "She's been taken."

"By who?" Chloe asked, now comfortable enough to come into the room, but not too close to me. Her phone remained in her hand.

"Another of my kind," I seethed, wings flexing as I remembered the figure I saw flying that night, and the ominous warning from The Mistress.

"What can we do?" Simon asked.

"Very little, I'm sure," a voice filled with tedium sighed behind me.

We all turned our attention to the demon in the room. Stefan, one gloved hand pinching the bridge of his nose as his eyes flicked from me to Simon, to Chloe, who met his gaze with a scream. Simon rushed to her side, putting an arm around her.

"That's what you scream at, not the moving statue, but the dude in cosplay?" Simon asked.

Stefan arched an eyebrow at Simon, then turned to me. "Your little scramble across the city drew eyes, gargoyle. The Mistress has rules for her domain, and you press your luck."

A roar tore from my chest as I took a step toward Stefan. "Henri is missing, taken!"

Stefan tilted his head, snapped, and caught the book that appeared in a whisper of smoke. Flipping the pages, he murmured to himself until he came to the page he was looking for. "Chloe Keita and Simon Laverda, your safety has already been bargained for."

"How do you know our names?" Chloe's voice trembled.

"What will you give me for the knowledge?" Stefan asked, a smile creeping across his face.

"No bargains tonight, demon," I spread a wing out, blocking the view between Stefan and the humans. "Do you know where Henri is?"

Stefan hummed. "I suppose I can give you this one for free, as you were both seen tearing through the sky tonight. Deal with it and I will let your transgressions go."

I snarled.

"Easy, gargoyle. Your enemy carried your human to the south side of the river. I suggest you keep your quarrel discreet, lest The Mistress get involved."

Snarling, I strode to the open window and stepped onto the ledge. The rain was falling heavier now, ruining what little visibility remained, and I had a lot of ground to cover if I was going to find Henri. Leaping off the edge, my wings snapped open, and I left just as I heard Stefan say behind me, "I suppose you two are coming with me for now."

South of the river. I'm coming, my stars. Please be safe.

# Chapter Twenty-Three

## Henri

Tall. Tall building. Was it swaying? Did I imagine that? Tall buildings sway, right? The wind wasn't helping, and neither was the rain as I huddled under the small overhang of the maintenance door. Several minutes ago, the strange gargoyle took several steps back, grinned, and flew away. Or hours, terror can make things feel like hours. Right?

*Ohhh, I'm going to need therapy for this.*

No phone, no pants for that matter, nothing to fend off the cold and the rain. Everything happened so fast, I didn't even know there was another gargoyle in Crossgate City. Did Zen know? Was Zen okay? I wasn't truly sure the droplets on my face were only rain anymore.

"Crap," I whimpered. Psyching myself up, I got on all fours and crawled out from under the overhang. My palms stung, the scraped skin still raw, as I made my way across the puddling rooftop. I couldn't get close to the edge. I couldn't make myself. No railing or fence separated the rooftop from the open sky around it. This area clearly wasn't meant to be accessed for much more than occasional technical issues. But I could see a lot more now than I could under the overhang. Not much more, thanks to a blanket of gray clouds covering the city, but more. It should have been obvious that there wouldn't be much traffic in the air, but without cars and pedestrians to sift through, it was at least easier to look for movement that could be Zendrax, or even the other gargoyle. Anything would be better than sitting in the rain, heart pounding, and anxiety climbing.

Movement caught my eye. A winged shape, I thought. "Zen?"

Hope crept into my voice, but there was no way he was going to hear me over this rain and wind. The figure swooped over another building, frantically searching. My heart hit my chest in a furious rhythm as I watched him, so far away and at the wrong buildings. Would he look here eventually? Would he see me in all this rain?

"Zen!" I called, but my voice sank to nothing in the heavy rain and whistling wind. His head turned for a moment, but whatever sound carried from me that his ears could pick up became lost as it bounced around the tall buildings. A fat tear rolled off my cheek, hotter than the chilled rain that pounded my back.

On shaky limbs, I positioned my feet under me and stood. Not too close to the edge, but far closer than my fear wanted.

Cupping my hands around my mouth, I yelled as loud as I could. "Zendrax!"

He stopped, looking around wildly. *Yes, that's it!*

"Zen!" I screamed, taking one step forward, and then he was able to lock in on my voice. My heart could have burst watching him twist through the air, making a beeline for my rooftop. Happy to sink to my knees, I was just glad this was over. I could warn him about the other gargoyle. I could—

Screams ripped through me as I felt myself shoved forward, my hands and knees not enough to keep me grounded on the solid roof as I flew several feet forward and toppled over the side. Absolute terror consumed me, the rush of air pressed in from all sides as the horror of free falling raced over my skin. A million thoughts vied for a turn as a rapid reflection of memories assaulted my mind. My mother not showing up to my first art show, the statue in the park near my childhood home that started me on the path to carving in the first place, the sketchbook from my art class where I met Simon, the last time I shared bubble tea with Chloe, and finally meeting Zen face to face on the rooftop.

The world tugged to the side, flipping my stomach like a flapjack as I registered the change in trajectory. My eyes, which had refused to focus on my impending doom, now met the jade stare of my savior. I couldn't even muster enough of my voice to say his name. I just flung my arms around Zen's neck with panicked tears. The rain pelted us with unforgiving drops that chilled to the bone. His arms tightened around me as he landed on a lower rooftop than where I had fallen from. Or, rather, pushed from.

"Gargoyle," I managed, the rambling beginning as I barely registered that I wasn't going to make much sense in this state. "Roof, my apartment. You were gone- I thought it was you! And he- we fell- And I thought I was gonna die and then I didn't, but we did it again!"

Zendrax pulled me closer, burying his face in the wet curls that clung to my neck. "I am here, my stars, and he will not touch you again."

I could hear wingbeats over the rain and wind, accompanied by the roar of distant thunder. With a growl, the strange gargoyle landed a short distance away.

Zen snapped his wings wide, shielding me from view and putting me to his back. And then everything froze as Zen stilled. "Uncle?"

*Uncle?*

The other gargoyle laughed darkly. "You should have taken an honorable death instead of banishment to this realm." He carried disgust in his words, and even though I couldn't see his face, I knew it must have been fierce from his tone.

My own muscles all seemed to bunch up, despite my shaking from cold and fear, and I hugged Zen from his back. He didn't deserve these cruel words, and from his remaining family, no less. His hand reached down to cover one of mine, his body relaxing just enough that I knew he felt my support.

"Now you've done it," a bored voice drawled from behind me. I jumped at the sound, then turned to see Stefan, using a large umbrella, standing in a circle of smoke that emanated from the ground. "I distinctly told you to keep your squabble low-profile."

The other gargoyle, Zen's uncle, roared in anger as he rushed forward to slash at Zendrax. I screamed at the action as my gargoyle defended himself with smooth precision while keeping himself between me and the attacker. Lightning cracked through the sky, and in the echoing boom of the thunder that accompanied it.

"You interfere in my domain." A commanding voice had me looking straight up at a vision of sin floating above us on leathery wings. Her skin was pale as the moon, except for the tips of her fingers, as well as her horns, which were black. Red eyes glowed like angry coals as she beheld the ants beneath her. Bat wings shredded through the back of her leather bodycon dress.

"A boon, demon!" Zen cried over the rising winds and rain. "Take her somewhere safe."

Demon, that's what she was. This had to be The Mistress. She tilted her head slowly, eyes moving behind me to Stefan as something silent passed between them.

"I will take her," Stefan answered.

"No!" I protested, but with Zen's back to me, there was nothing to argue with, and I turned to Stefan.

A disturbingly wide grin spread across his face, highlighting a mouth filled with sharpened teeth I hadn't noticed before. "I accept your deal, gargoyle."

Stefan made a pulling motion with one gloved hand and my body began to move, as if being sucked up by a vacuum. Digging my heels into the rooftop on instinct, the scrape against my bare heels hurt too much to continue resisting for long. Protesting the entire way, Zen kept his back to me, his wings spread wide.

"I will return to you, my stars," he promised.

"Zen!" I shouted one more time before Stefan placed a hand on my shoulder.

"The Mistress will deal with this swiftly, gargoyle. I will uphold my end of the deal. You may collect her from The Crossroads when you are done." In a whoosh of smoke, the gray clouds that ringed the place where Stefan was standing billowed up to block everything around us from view. In a heartbeat, my body felt weightless and my stomach lurched as if being tossed around on a wild carnival ride until we landed somewhere soft.

As I tumbled forward, red carpet met my hands and knees. A racing heart grounded me as I reoriented myself. The rooftop was gone. The rain was gone. Then the smoke cleared, and I could feel Stefan's presence beside me.

"Henri!" A pair of brown hands were the first thing to enter my sight as Chloe all but hauled me to my feet and pulled me into a hug. "You're shivering. We need to get you dried off."

As Chloe spoke, the room filled out. We stood in some kind of bedroom, or at least there was a bed in it, which I noticed just before finding the wall of toys. There was suggestive artwork scattered everywhere, and one entire wall was made up of mirrored panels.

"The Crossroads," I murmured as a large, warm tear rolled down my cheek. Recovering my lungs, I turned to Stefan. "Take me back!" I demanded.

"I can't do that," he answered, tugging one of his gloves into place.

"Please!" I shrieked as Chloe kept her arms around me. "Zen's in trouble!"

"Let me rephrase that," Stefan calmly said, leveling his gaze on me. "I cannot break the boundaries of the deal I just made with Zendrax any more than you could remove your head and carry it around with you. You will be kept safe here, just as he requested."

Chloe came down onto the carpet with me as I sank to the floor, and a pair of boots appeared at the corner of my eye. Simon crouched down on my other side and soothingly rubbed a hand on my back.

"I will send something for you to wear," Stefan said, walking towards the door before pausing. "And I suppose I can offer you this one solace."

He waved his hand, and the mirrored wall appeared to fill with smoke. Stefan left, and the first sobs racked my body while my friends held me. When Chloe sucked in a sharp breath, I looked up, finding the mirrors projecting moving images as though they were a television.

Tonight's program: two gargoyles in a fight to the death.

# Chapter Twenty-Four

## Zendrax

The contract demon's presence vanished behind me, along with my heart. With him went Henri, the human responsible for scraping the remnants of my heart back together. The devastation of the battle, the loss of my kin and clan, the banishment from my home. I wasn't sure I would survive it, and until recently, I didn't care if I did.

But my uncle's betrayal would not go unanswered.

"You raise your wings to me, Havaxus?" I demanded, my voice thundering with the skies as rain fell around us.

"I come to finish what should have been done!" he snarled, the hatred on his face an unrecognizable mask from the family I had known my whole life.

"Out." The command echoed painfully in my mind, and from his expression, my uncle as well. Risking a glance upward, the demoness who had granted me asylum to her domain was wrath incarnate. Wings I had never seen before held her aloft, and her eyes were a glowing forge, ready to cast damnation upon us.

"Mistress," I began.

"*Out*." The demoness of Crossgate City raised her arms. Her blackened fingertips lit like the red coals of her eyes as she slashed her hand through the sky, prying open a smoking window through the air between Havaxus and myself.

Registering the red cliffs and deep gorge through the portal, I sucked in a breath at the sight of my homeland. Before I could register the symphony of emotions that shot through my heart, an unseen force shoved me through the portal. Weightless, breathless, falling. Through the smoke, through the sky. As I tumbled, I found the stars I never thought I'd see again and snapped my wings wide to catch the air. Hitting the ground, my claws dug through the red dust as I halted myself, looking for Havaxus. He landed similarly, just a few wingspans away. We were nowhere near the castle, or the gorge, for that matter. All around us stretched nothing but the open fields of the barren lands.

"What have you done?" I screamed, my heart torn between the homeland I never thought I'd lay eyes upon again, and the home I had come to love. An entirely new world, where I healed the wounds of my lost family and friends. Where I repented my failure. Where I found Henri.

"You care for the realm of those demons?" Havaxus sneered. "It matters little. I found you, and now I will finish you."

He lunged, claws extending to slash at my throat. Jumping back, I roared my defiance. "Why seek me out? What do you gain?"

"Gain?" His eyes flashed with wrath. "The clan moans and mourns your loss. The loss of one who failed them! Your banishment gave them hope of your return, a call to change our ways. I knew I should have waited longer to come to the battle, when I would find your stones crumbled with Tava's. Even your sisters, Vrya and Wyrva, fell at her side, and yet you were allowed the shame of living?" Havaxus spat in the dirt at my feet.

My head spun with the implications of his declaration, but I refused to show a reaction to his slight. "What do you mean you waited, Havaxus?"

He lunged again, this time catching me off guard, slashing my shoulder as I failed to dodge his attack in time. A roar erupted from me, fury and pain and sorrow all at once. "Tell me what you meant!"

His silence screamed between us. Havaxus, my mother's twin, had known somehow. Had known we battled that day, but did not come to his twin's aid. Overhead, wingbeats distracted us for a mere moment before Havaxus and I circled one another. The moment an opening showed itself, we would jump into a deadly entanglement.

What did he gain at the loss of his sister's clan? No, not the loss of the entire clan. Just the loss of its leader. What he gained was more territory, the scraps of our clan. My clan.

"Havaxus," my voice evened with clarity. "Betrayer. Coward. You *waited* for my mother to die."

The wingbeats from a moment ago descended, lowering around us as clawed feet hit the ground. I didn't dare take my eyes off my uncle, but the voices were familiar as each spoke.

"Zendrax! We saw the lights in the sky, your fall to the ground. What is going on?" my cousin cried. A terrible mix of thoughts swirled within me in the span of a heartbeat. Was Nyzax a betrayer as well, or was he blissfully unaware of his father's betrayal?

"What is this about, Tava?" Marzav asked. The elder who had saved my life with his knowledge of the humans' research. Havaxus hissed, "Do not listen to the mutterings of a banished failure!"

"How have you returned?" Marzav asked, ignoring my uncle's words.

Nyzax stepped forward, not quite daring to enter our slow circling as Havaxus and I stared one another down with deadly promise. "Cease this. Father, what are you doing? Why do you fight Zendrax?"

"He is banished!" Havaxus was now screaming. "He forfeits his banishment, and now must be crumbled for his failure to protect the castle!"

Nyzax looked as though his father had struck him. "What is happening? Zen, how are you here?"

I broke eye contact with my uncle just long enough to see my cousin, brother of my heart. "He waited, Zax. He waited for my mother to die before he came to help."

Nyzax could not have known. The raw pain that washed over him began as disbelief, but slowly spread from his face down to the rest of his body. His eyes darted to empty points between us as his mind raced through the events of that day. "No . . ." he started, but his words failed him.

"Don't listen to him," Havaxus demanded. "I am the leader of the clan now. You will listen to me!"

We clashed, claw and tooth and wing and tail. I roared with pain as Havaxus took advantage of the wound he'd made in my shoulder, scoring the lines deeper. At the first opportunity, I struck back, raking down his side with my claws. Jumping back from each other, if only to catch our breath, we lunged again. The encircling gargoyles protested, demanding answers.

"Father!" Nyzax demanded. "This can't be. Stop this fight and answer us!"

"Havaxus," Marzav echoed, "we cannot solve this unless you stop and speak to your people." Many voices joined him in agreement. The corners of my vision revealed familiar faces, ones I wasn't able to confirm the survival of after the battle that felled Stoneforge Castle. My jaw tightened as I strained to keep my eyes locked on Havaxus. How many nights had I lost wondering what had happened to many of these gargoyles?

"Havaxus, the betrayer." My chest ached with every word. "You are unfit to guide this clan of gargoyles, and I challenge you for your wings."

Roars of astonishment, gasps, murmurs all circled where my uncle and I faced each other.

"Cousin," Nyzax began, "Father, defend yourself! Say it isn't true. Tell him the delays were true, that you came as fast as you could."

Havaxus could have done so. He could have swayed his son, who was breaking apart. He could have convinced the elders with his words. But Havaxus had reached the end of his temperament, and I could see in his gaze the moment he snapped.

"Tava was no leader!" he roared. "It should have been me!"

Rushing forward, he met my challenge head on. Crashing into one another, we met. His claws collided with my sides and dug in as I did the same.

"Coward!" I roared. "Traitor!"

"Weakling!" he screamed back. "Disgrace!"

"Father!" Nyzax began, but I could see Marzav and one of the elder female warriors hold him back.

Havaxus pushed back from me, tail lashing as he launched for my legs to topple me. My wings snapped out just in time to catch my weight, moving me backward before I threw myself forward to pin him to the rough ground. A long gash of claw-marks across his neck and shoulder was my reward until Havaxus rolled me from him and kicked me in the stomach.

The gathered gargoyles were shouting, crying in outrage or lament for the revelation of their leader's betrayal. But I was in no conflict. Havaxus had orchestrated my family's death, my clan's defeat, and my Henri's abduction. He would not live to create one more wrong.

My uncle, for all his misdeeds, was still a seasoned warrior. If I wanted to claim his wings, as I had threatened, I would have to calculate a loss. Swallowing, I begged Henri's forgiveness if I did not make it back to her realm, then kicked off the red dirt toward Havaxus.

Crashing together, I left my side open as I placed all my faith into my long reach as I scooped one arm up under the side of his ribs to grab the base of a wing. Pain exploded at my side, but when my fingers wrapped around the joint that would connect wing to body, I seized the moment. I couldn't catch my breath with Havaxus' claws in my side, but I still put all the strength I had into pulling that joint until I felt it strain, then snap. The crack of stone echoed in the dry, open plains as the gargoyles around us instantly silenced. Havaxus roared in pain and rage, as this was something that no amount of sunning would grow back. The highest shame to a gargoyle warrior.

"Havaxus!" I cried. "You are not fit to lead these gargoyles."

Havaxus pushed himself from me, and, as his claws left my side, I fell to a knee, grasping at the center of the pain. The sluggish ooze of bodily fluids seeped through, filling the long cracks, but under my hands I could already feel that too much had been dug away, and I too would be missing crevices of stone come tomorrow.

"Havaxus of Stoneforge Castle and the Grand Gate," Nyzax had found his voice again, broken anew with sorrow. "You are found unfit to lead. Take him away to be judged by the elders. The fates have failed him in a challenge for his wings."

The scene Havaxus made was shameful. Lashing out, even as several warriors surrounded him, escorting him away. There was no solace on display, and my heart ached deeply again for my mother and sisters. This disgrace was his own, but even in avenging his wrongdoings, I could not bring back my kin.

A hand landed gently on my shoulder. Marzav.

"I had questions for our new leader, after the dust of battle settled," he said. "I can see now why he avoided them. This will be a great shock to us all."

"Zendrax, I know not what to say. The shame of my family to yours is insurmountable." Nyzax joined us, kneeling in front of me. "If anyone has a right to lead the clan, it is you."

One by one, the warriors who remained joined Nyzax on their knees, heads bowed, wings drawn in. Faces I had not seen for half a year held emotions I could scarcely judge. But I was not the same warrior that left them. The growth I experienced in the new realm had changed me.

"I could not bear the task of it, cousin," I told him softly. "Lift your head, all of you. While Havaxus was indeed a betrayer, the truth that my family and I were unable to protect our clan in battle remains the same."

Nyzax stood, lending a hand to pull me up as well. "Zendrax, what are you saying?"

What was I saying? It took another look at each face surrounding me to know what I wanted to do. "While my love for you and this land is great, so is my pain. I will be returning to the realm to which I was banished."

The murmurs that strung through the gargoyles were a low hush, like the wind. Faces held pain, understanding, respect, and more. Grasping my cousin's hands, we held a firm gaze between us. "It must be you. You already have the hearts of our people and were always meant to be a leader."

"Stay, please," he asked.

"I cannot." Bowing my head, I no longer had the strength to face him. To face any of them.

And the silence stretched.

"If you cannot stay," said a voice beside me, "then I will go with you."

My head lifted in a blink. "Marzav, do not banish yourself alongside me."

He shrugged one wing, and the elder scratched his beard. "I have no fledglings of my own, Zendrax. Watching you, Vrya, and Wyrva grow up was a joy for many of us. And you dangle the promise of an entirely new realm in front of a scholar. How do you expect him not to have a glint in his eye for it?" Marzav broke the tension as laughter accompanied his words.

"I do not know what to say." My throat tightened. "You will owe The Mistress a payment of some kind to come, but there are more than enough buildings to roost."

Nyzax patted my back. "Come back to the clan. First, we inform all of what happened here. Then we sort out your return to this new realm."

"Agreed," Marzav said. "For the return of Tava's son, we should feast!"

# Chapter Twenty-Five

## Henri

"Spill," Chloe said in one ear.

"All of it," Simon chimed in from the other.

The bed sank as each of them took a seat next to me. My hands pulled the silk robe tightly around my body, attempting to warm up from the rain. Two of the gold-collared employees from The Crossroads had brought us in hot drinks, snacks, and dried me off before stuffing me in a robe. They almost had me naked before I managed to scream that I wanted to change in the bathroom, but even that wasn't a solo activity as they took care of my soaked hair. But the second I had a robe on, I opened the door, and my eyes remained glued on the fight.

Zen's uncle. I was used to my family letting me down, sure, but this? It looked like the other gargoyle really wanted to kill him. My heart ached watching every blow, every kick, every swipe of claw or bite of fang. Everything in me was crying out to help, but besides the fact that getting in the way could be deadly, we were in two different planes of existence now.

"Hen?" Chloe said, snapping me out of it.

"Right, yeah, explanation," I murmured, then we all winced as Zen's uncle slashed at his shoulder.

"I'm sure he's fine," Simon said. "He's a giant rock of muscle. Back to the conversation. I think we need to straighten out some facts."

Blinking, I pulled my eyes from the mirrored wall that Stefan had turned into my own personal suspense flick. "What do you want to know?"

"How the hell did you meet a *gargoyle*?" Simon asked.

Chloe rubbed a hand up and down my back. "I think you told us, didn't you? Back at the tea shop."

"Oh, you mean when I tried to tell you, and you wanted to convince me it was a maintenance guy?" I gestured to the mirror. "There he is! There's my maintenance guy!"

"Alright, fine," Chloe groaned. "It wasn't a maintenance guy. Can you still give us some details? Because we walked into your apartment—"

"With Sawadees," Simon added.

"You went to Sawadees?" I protested.

"Focus." Chloe pinched the bridge of her nose and closed her eyes. "We walked in with dinner, and found you gone, and a giant, moving statue looking for you."

My eyes drifted back to the wall where Zen was circling his uncle, but now I could see other gargoyles around them. "Zen is . . . we're together."

"I knew it!" Simon added. "I saw your drawings."

Nodding, I pulled the robe tighter, then flinched when the gargoyles exchanged more blows. This mirror magic was more detailed than any screen I'd seen before, and it was agonizing.

"How did that even happen? Do you," Chloe paused, "have you—"

"Not now, Chlo," Simon said. "If Henri cares about him, that's all I need to know. *For now.*"

Sighing through my nose, I pulled my eyes off the wall long enough to hold Chloe's hand. "This place is run by someone called The Mistress. She made a deal with Zen. To bring him here and leave his home. There was a fight, some drama—"

"Obviously." Simon snorted.

Chloe glared at him. "Go on, Henri."

The conflict in the mirror came to a head. Other gargoyles had joined them, and it appeared they were shouting. Zen and his uncle circled one another, lashing out where they had openings until they came to a final clash.

"Zen!" I jumped off the bed, skipping Chloe's question entirely as I pressed my hands to the mirror. Horror and fascination gripped my throat as my breath came high and tight.

"Brutal," Simon commented as the three of us watched Zendrax tear off his uncle's wing. To them, it was no different from seeing a movie. They didn't really know Zen. But I couldn't tear my eyes from the deep gashes in his side where his uncle had wounded him in the same moment. It was a clear victory, but at the cost of deep injuries.

Sinking to the floor, my unblinking gaze wouldn't release me from the image of Zen surrounded by his clan.

Footsteps cushioned by the plush carpet made their way to my side as Chloe crouched down next to me. "Your guy won."

"He did," I murmured.

"Then why do you look so upset?" she prodded.

Was I? Taking note of my body, everything was tense. My hands were balled into fists, my shoulders were stiff. Letting out a slow breath, I collected why I was so affected by this.

"Two things," I offered. "First, Zen is hurt. And second . . ."

"He's back home," Simon said.

My mouth went dry, and I offered a slow nod. "He's back where his home is."

We watched for a few heartbeats while I processed what I was seeing. He was so happy to be with them, I could see it on his face. What I wouldn't give to hear what they were saying.

Zendrax looked up, searching the sky for something, and I leaned back from the mirrored wall.

"He's looking for something," Simon said.

"He's looking for his way back," Chloe added.

Standing, I pressed my palm against the glass, the cold surface a flush contrast to the fire under my skin. Zen, for whatever reason, still wanted to come back. The draw of his own people, his home, still didn't stop him from looking up at the sky.

Sprinting as fast as my legs would take me, I held my robe in a death grip at my chest and flung open the door to the club.

"Where are you going?" I barely heard Chloe behind me as I dashed through the hallway filled with provocative sconces and lingerie-clad workers with those gold collars. But none of them knew what was going on, and I needed a familiar face.

The hall opened to the larger room, and my eyes locked onto Tanya, working at the bar. Her eyes widened as I nearly slammed into the magnificent marble counter and blurted out, "Stefan! He's coming back. I want to make a deal!"

She quickly slipped an amber glass to a giant, scaly guy before giving me her full attention as she slipped out from behind the bar.

"Slow down. What is happening?" she asked.

"Zen! He—The fight!" I flung my index finger toward the room. "Zen won. He needs to come back. I want to make a deal, and I need Stefan!"

"What's this about a deal?" A low tone purred in my ear, and I spun around and looked up into the intimidating gaze of The Mistress.

"Mistress." Tanya bowed her head.

This was Stefan's boss, the head demon in charge. Zen already made a deal with Stefan, so I kind of knew how this worked, but my heart still hammered as I committed to the words that spilled from my lips. "I want to make a deal to bring Zendrax back to this realm!"

Her eyes, glowing red coals surrounded by black depths, settled on me with a pause. The gold jewelry that adorned her fingers and horns glinted in the lights of the club as she tilted her head and tapped her chin.

"And what is it a human could possibly offer me for the effort? You have not even brought me a boon for my time," she said coolly.

My eyes slid to Tanya, who pointed to the high shelf of bottles.

"A tab. Can I open a tab?" I asked.

Tanya nodded. "I have a nicely aged scotch, if you're looking for recommendations. Dry, with a sprig of mint."

The Mistress and her impeccably painted lips quirked upward. "Don't be pert, Tanya."

"I'll take it," I said, and the bartender was quickly sliding a glass in my direction. "For your time, please," I addressed the demoness in front of me.

The Mistress leaned over, gazing into the glass for a moment before raising it to her lips with a smile. "Go on, human. What is it you wish to offer me for such a task?"

My eyes had already been darting around the club, and I'd noticed something since the first time I set food in the space. The Mistress was a collector. "My art."

She set the glass on the bar, lifting one eyebrow. "Your art?"

"Yes," I said, without hesitation. I was fidgeting with the collar of my robe, unable to keep my nervous fingers from moving. "I'm a sculptor. I would like to make you a piece. I think I have a good idea of your preferred subject matter, and I can deliver it within six months."

Her eyes lit up. "I approve, human. You have yourself a bargain."

Sagging in relief, I steadied myself with a hand on the bar. "Oh, thank goodness."

"Just know, human," the demoness purred, licking a drop of scotch from the corner of her mouth as her glowing red eyes drifted up and down my form. "A bargain with me is more than a promise of words. Be sure to uphold your end of it." She waved a hand and carried her glass of whisky away from the bar. "Tanya, see to it these humans are comfortable enough while they wait. I will bring the gargoyle back before night's end."

The threat was noted. I could have cried as I sank into the bar with shaky legs. Tanya came around from behind it once more to help steady me. "Come on, let's get you back to your friends."

Tanya opened the door to the mirror room, framing Chloe as she paced past Simon, who leaned against a non-mirrored wall. I was relieved to see Zendrax, still displayed in the glass, being welcomed peacefully by the other gargoyles.

"Henri," Chloe said. "Where did you go?"

Tanya swept into the room, leaving me with little choice but to follow her. "Henri was securing the gargoyle's way home," Tanya answered, walking straight to a closet.

"What does that mean?" Simon asked, pushing off the wall and walking toward me with his face pinched tight.

"Zen can come home," I answered as we watched Tanya rifle through the closet. "In exchange, I'm making a sculpture to the owner's taste."

Chloe eyed a painting on the wall. "I can imagine what that might be."

"Henri, what size bra do you wear?" Tanya asked, leaning out of the closet with a bunch of ribbon in her fist that couldn't possibly count as a garment.

"Bra? Why?" I sputtered.

"Eh, you're right, no need for a bra. Let me see if we have any of those chains clean," she said, diving back in.

"What in the world are you doing now?" Chloe asked.

"Dressing Henri for her lover's return to the realm," Tanya answered with nonchalance. She scrunched her lips to one side of her face. "Humans, are you two alright being sent home now? All dry, refreshed, ensured that Henri will be alright?"

Chloe and Simon exchanged a nervous look.

"I know I owe you so much more of an explanation," I offered my best friends. "But I think everything really will be okay for now. We can get coffee tomorrow and I'll tell you everything. Or we can get takeout and bring it back to my place, and I'll introduce you to Zen properly."

Chloe still shifted a look at Tanya. "Are you sure you want whatever this one has in mind for you, Hen?"

The succubus was still rifling through supplies in the closet as I chewed my lip. Watching her dig for mysterious items, I responded to Chloe, "I'm not quite sure what she's up to, but I can deal with that. I'm perfectly safe and comfortable here with Tanya. Promise."

Chloe bit her lower lip before striding the distance between us, pulling me into a hug. "If you're sure."

"Positive," I answered, hugging her back.

Simon slung an arm around my shoulder. "I'll get Chloe home. Text when you're back safe, okay?"

Chloe waved Simon off. "I don't even have it in me to chastise you for assuming I need to be taken home. I've got the chills from everything I've seen tonight."

Tanya pulled herself out of the closet long enough to whistle toward the door, then nodded in our direction. "After everything you've been through, I don't blame anyone for being overwhelmed. But no one is seeing anyone else home, except for one of our people. You deserve that much, at least."

A big man opened the door. Blond hair, shaved on one side and ending past his shoulders on the other, he was enormous. A pegasus took up the better half of his left arm.

Recognition hit me instantly, but I had forgotten his name since he helped me find The Crossroads that first night. "Hi, um . . ."

"Ivor. Nice to see you've acclimated here." The big man winked, then he turned to Tanya. "Did you need something?"

"Take a couple humans home?" Tanya asked. "They've been through a lot, and I would appreciate it."

Ivor laughed, opening the door wider. "Anything for you, but if you're feeling gracious, I accept tips in shots."

"Thank you," Chloe said to Tanya, but smiling up at Ivor. "It's been a long day."

They said their goodbyes with one last crushing hug from Chloe, and my friends were safely on the way to their respective homes. It was a load off my shoulders that I didn't know was there, but with nothing left to focus on, I shut the door behind them and turned to Tanya, who was back in the closet.

"So, what *are* you doing?" I asked.

Tanya pulled herself from the closet, holding an armful of different fabrics. "If there's one thing I know about big, strong, warrior types, it's that once they've tasted a victory, they're ready for an entirely different sort of conquest."

The devilish grin on her face as she strutted toward me was alarming enough that I took a step back. "Conquest? Oh. OH!"

"I think I about have your measurements worked out, but let me put you into something a little less . . ." she shrugged, offering me no apology in the toothy grin she wore. "A little less."

# Chapter Twenty-Six

## Zendrax

Stone surrounded me. At my side was my cousin, at my back was my clan, and at my feet was the field of the fallen. Crumbled gargoyles who had fallen in honorable battle slumbered here, as still as if the sun were shining. But there would be no dusk to awaken them, not this time.

"The night is long, Zendrax," Nyzax said, placing a hand on my shoulder.

"We laid everyone to sun for the last time with the highest honors we could," Marzav offered.

Nodding at their words, I felt my heart tearing. Bits and pieces of friends and family, of brothers and sisters in arms. The knowledge that they were now at peace, high up in the stars above, consoled me, but the disgraceful betrayal that placed so many in this field for the last time sat ill in my chest.

A rumble opened in the sky behind us. Looking over my shoulder, I could see the clouds rolling low and dark as they blotted out the bright specks of light in the night sky. It did nothing more than remind me of the evening storms I'd enjoyed from Henri's window, and my heart felt heavy.

"You need to go back," Nyzax offered. "The others are finishing the feast, packing the remainder for our journey."

My brow furrowed. "Journey?"

Marzav laughed. "You thought our words a jest, Zendrax? Many of us, myself in particular, wish to make our own bargains to join you in this new realm. The deceit of this new human kingdom, having conspired with your uncle, does not sit well with us."

"No," Nyzax's face darkened. "It does not."

Studying my cousin's face, I wished to know his thoughts. But it wasn't my place to pry, as I was the one who had unveiled Havaxus in his plotting. The cause of his current disgrace was me. I turned to the gargoyles around us, many of them casting their eyes upon the field where our loved ones laid in rest. Were they remembering that fateful battle? Did they still mourn the loss, more so now that the betrayal was unmasked?

Lifting my head, my wings, I spoke to them. "I am told some of you wish to come to the realm of Crossgate. I will not lie. This place is difficult to understand at first. But for those who wish to leave this shameful kingdom behind to serve another roost, I offer what help I can. I will bargain with The Mistress for your passage."

Agreement rumbled around us. Heads nodded as hands clasped with their neighbors in a sign of unity. A mix of members, some from each clan, stood with marked determination to leave and forge new footing.

"We are with you, Zendrax," Marzav offered, clapping a hand to my shoulder.

"And you, cousin?" I turned to Nyzax.

His posture was stiff, his shoulders tense. "I cannot. Someone must stay with those who wish to remain. This is the only home many of us have known." He lifted his head, his expression tainted with sorrow. "I will keep them safe. We may even leave, back to the gate. The walls of this keep no longer feel right."

Silence stretched between us. My memories of all the time spent together playing, training, exploring, fishing. There was no swaying my cousin's mind once he set it. And what cause was more noble than caring for our kin and clan? Still . . .

"If a day comes when you would join me in Crossgate, I would welcome you with open arms."

He smiled at that. "I will keep it in my heart, cousin."

Marzav clapped. "Then come! I will prepare a suitable prize to entice The Mistress to hear our request. Say your goodbyes, collect your things, we meet at the top of the gorge with haste."

Good. Now we could all leave the time for sorrows behind us. I could now return to my home, my heart, my stars. And I would bring my kin with me.

The dusty room of long-dead scholars was much the same. Someone, likely Marzav, had tidied the loose scrolls and books. And a blessing that was, because soon every spare bit of ground held a waiting gargoyle, ready to leave this world behind them. The remaining members of my former clan were coming, including the fledglings. A handful of our sister clan joined us as well, swelling our numbers to the dozens. I briefly wondered if our presence would be too large for the city itself, but if some of us took to the nearby mountains, it should be no problem.

"Are we all ready?" Marzav asked, setting several bottles of alcohol and a silver smoking pipe in front of the lines that would make up the portal—if The Mistress answered our call, that is.

Agreement echoed through the lot of us, and Marzav performed the same ritual he had before. Grunts of caution and curiosity accompanied the smoke that languidly traced the lines that would become the doorway.

I began shifting my weight with impatience. How long had I been here? Hours? And how much time had passed in Crossgate? Henri was probably worried, and while I wouldn't leave my people right after appearing before them to open their wounds of grief afresh, I couldn't stay away from Henri, either. The Mistress had to appear, she must. Otherwise, I didn't know how to get back to my stars and dry any tears she may have shed on my undeserving behalf.

The smoke thickened, and out stepped The Mistress. Her stunning presence caused an anxious breath to escape me. Eyes like red-hot coals with black centers swept across the room. Her lips parted as she lifted her pipe to meet them. She wore a dress this time, long and black, with slits up to her waist over each hip, dripping with cold jewelry.

"Zendrax, was it?" she asked, then looked down at her feet to the offerings, which elicited a smile. "Another deal then."

"What is she saying?" someone murmured behind me, and I remembered the first time when she cast some sort of magic over us to allow speech.

"Mistress," I began, "Not all of us can understand your words. If you will allow it, I would request the same bewitchment as before, so we can do business."

Tilting her head, she took another drag from her pipe and let out a slow ribbon of smoke. Lifting her free hand, she snapped those ink-black fingers and all but Marzav and myself grunted or gasped at the sensation.

"Better?" she drawled, leaning over to pick up the silver pipe with interest.

"Mistress," Marzav bowed his head. "We wish to relocate to the realm where you took Zendrax before."

She raised an eyebrow, tucking the silver pipe between her breasts, allowing the larger end to stick out the top of her dress as she picked up the first bottle of liquor. "All of you?"

"If you will it, yes," I confirmed. "I wish to take on a boon to you for each of my kin and kind. Serving tasks to you, if you will accept these terms to bring all of us to Crossgate City."

"No!" Marzav protested, and agreement echoed from the others in the room. "This is our own choice, and a deal we must each make. You can't give anymore, not for our sakes."

The Mistress held up a hand, silencing the protests. "A deal has been struck, though not by you, Zendrax."

Brows lowered, I clenched my fists. "What do you mean?" Something felt off, and I didn't do well with the unexpected. The fate of my people would not be in the hands of another.

Her eyes crinkled, amusement dancing on her lips. "The exchange of one portal for Zendrax of Stoneforge has been negotiated for by one Henrietta Prichard."

Everything stilled. What had she given up for my sake? "Henri?"

The Mistress tucked her chosen bottle under one arm before leaning down to retrieve another. "I am not in the habit of repeating myself, gargoyle."

"What does this mean?" Marzav asked, turning to me."

I didn't have an answer, other than the assurance of my own passage. "Mistress, what of the passage for the rest of my kin and clan?"

She shrugged, still studying the newest bottle of libations. "A collective boon, then. Your kind are protectors, yes? There are places they can go, and you can keep a few in Old Town with you. In exchange, every one of them will follow the rules. And, should a time come when the city is in need of defending . . ."

Too simple, it was almost too easy. My people were made for this very thing, to defend the land and keep our watchful eyes for battle. This was no task at all, but the way of life we had always maintained. It was on Marzav's face as well, and a few others near enough for me to glance at. Whatever Henri had traded, whatever deal she had struck, must have pleased The Mistress greatly.

"You have our word," I said. "And our protection. It will take time to settle everyone in and explain the ways of the realm, but you have our word." Agreement from my back reassured my decision.

She smiled, gesturing to the bottles still at her feet and placing the one she had just picked up in Marzav's unexpecting hands. "Be a dear and carry those, will you? I will bring you all to your new home."

Smoke swirled in the air as the nearest hands followed The Mistress's orders, grabbing her gifts, sealing our deal with her. We were coming home to Crossgate.

# Chapter Twenty-Seven

## Henri

It had been hours, but I could wait. I saw Zen having a moment with his people in the mirror before the effects Stefan had placed on the glass surface receded. It was a simple mirror once again, leaving me with no way to know what Zendrax was doing, aside from the fact that he had won his fight.

Tanya had dressed me in something of a bra and panties set. If you could call red mesh held together by threads and optimism a bra and panty set. A farce of a robe, made of black lace in the shape of bat wings—something I suspected was an ode to Zendrax's own—attempted to cover me to mid-thigh. There was even a polished end table with an assortment of items on them, but I didn't have the curiosity in me to bother looking through anything while Zen was still on my mind. Tanya insisted everything was going to be "gratifying" to my specific tastes, and I didn't question it. Since finding out she was a succubus, I wasn't sure how many details I really wanted from her.

The agonizing wait passed with wild theories spinning through my head. What if Zen didn't want to come back? What if he now had his people's forgiveness, and he wanted to stay with them? Or what if The Mistress changed her mind about the deal, and she demanded more favors from Zen? Or what if—my thoughts stopped as the door was opened by Tanya's hand.

"Enjoy," she purred, giving me a wink before disappearing down the hall as a large, gray figure replaced her in the doorway.

"Zen!" I jolted off the bed, throwing my arms around his neck as he lifted me into a tight hug.

"My stars." He pressed his face into my neck, breathing me in even as my fingertips traced over the parts of him I'd seen get hurt through the mirror.

"Your side, is your side okay? Stefan turned the wall into a screen, and I saw the whole fight." The surface was definitely still gouged. But where his uncle had dug his claws into Zen's side, there was now a cool pooling of what felt like fresh cement that hadn't dried quite yet. The area was very smooth, with a slight bounce-back when I touched it.

Zen sucked in a breath through his teeth, gently peeling my hand away. "Tender, but only if you touch that spot directly. I would otherwise not notice it."

"Sorry!" I clutched the offending hand to my chest. "Sorry, you usually have less feeling in your skin than I do. Can I help? Does it need to be cleaned or bandaged?"

Zen shook his head, setting me down on my feet even as he placed a hand on my back to walk with me to the bed. "A few days of sunning will solve the problem, and it will heal as much as the skies will it."

"The sun, shouldn't it be up soon?" I asked, sitting on the bed as Zen crouched in front of it to better match my height.

"There are two or three hours yet, my stars." He reached out, one claw tracing the ribbon which held the sorry excuse of a robe closed. "Right now, I am more interested in reuniting with you. Havaxus took you. You must have been frightened. I have failed you on my promise to keep you safe."

My heart leapt into my throat, the sudden remembrance of what I was wearing mixed with Zen taking this as a failure. He looked so upset with himself that I found my hand reaching to cup his jaw, my thumb caressing his cheek. "You haven't! I mean, I was afraid when he took me, but you saved me. It was amazing to watch you fight, but I was more worried about you than me the whole time. Everyone here took care of me."

His expression only darkened. "You made a deal in my stead, Henri. You shouldn't do that."

"Of course I did that! I couldn't stand the thought of you owing her another scary river monster favor, or something even worse. And if it meant bringing you home, I had to do something."

He was quiet for a moment, placing his hand over mine against his face, as though he was trying to take all the warmth from my skin. "What was your offer to the portal demon?"

"Art. A sculpture. I have a pretty good sense of her tastes at this point." Looking to the wall, at the chosen artwork, and Zen's eyes followed mine to a painting of three women in the most entangled, erotic position I'd ever seen.

Zen let out a breath, closing his eyes. "Do not frighten me again, my stars. I don't know what I would do if you found trouble because of me."

Pulling my hand free from his, I used it to adjust my weight on the mattress until I was on my knees, leaning forward. "I don't mind finding trouble if it means helping you. You're the best part of my nights, you're my muse. You're kind and smart, and at least one of us knows how to cook."

Zen chuckled at that, leaning forward until our foreheads met.

"I love you, Zen," I whispered, moving my forehead back to reach up and kiss his.

He stilled. "Henri . . ." In one motion, he was on his feet, pulling me into his arms for an embrace, only deepening when our lips found each other. My arms went around his neck while his fingers entwined with the hair at the back of my head. We pulled apart, my breaths coming quick and shallow.

"I love you as well, my stars," Zen confessed. "You have become the hearth that I come home to, the light in my night's sky."

"Zen," I choked, and we kissed again. "Thank you for coming back. For a minute there, I was getting in my own head. That you might stay there with the other gargoyles, and I couldn't even blame you if you did."

His expression twisted into mischief. "I will tell you everything, but later. Now that I am back, and you are laid before me like a treasure to unwrap, I feel we can shift our focus to other matters."

"What is that supposed to *m*—!" Zen had me on my back before I knew it, peppering my neck with kisses even as one hand began gently tugging at the ribbon of my robe.

"The pink one gave me very specific instructions on the supplies she left in this room," Zen teased, taking my bottom lip between sharp teeth for a gentle tug. "Suggestions I would very much like to see played out on your body, if you're willing."

My eyes roamed over the table at the foot of the bed. A bucket of ice, half a dozen flickering tapered candles, a bowl of metal pieces I couldn't figure out the use of, a stack of towels, and a blindfold.

But this was Zen, and whatever they were for, I figured Tanya knew what she was talking about. Further, I had all the faith in the world that this gargoyle wouldn't hurt me.

*Or at least that he wouldn't hurt me in a way I don't like.*

"Yes," I breathed, "do it."

"You need only to tell me to stop if you dislike anything," he offered, undoing a battle-tattered kilt and tossing it to the floor. "May I blindfold you?"

Laughing, I nodded before he picked up the black satin cloth. "You're a bit too polite for someone who I suspect is supposed to put me through a bit of torture."

"Ah, but it will be blissful torture, my stars." He fixed the cloth comfortably around my eyes, ensuring that it didn't pinch anywhere or allow any sight through. Shaped a little like a sleep mask, the padding over my eyes helped turn the world to a pitch black.

My choices were not my own as I relied on Zen to move me where he wanted; more centered on the bed. My heart was racing as my ears became my new favored sense for telling what was going on. For something so big and heavy, his footsteps gave nothing away. His damn arms were so long he probably didn't need to move to reach the table, so the only clues I had as to what he could have reached for came in the form of soft clinks as his claw-tipped fingers explored the options. He picked through the metal pieces, and then I heard the ice cubes as they clinked together in their bowl. Zen was taking his sweet time.

"I have always liked how you react to my touch when I come in after a cold rain, my stars." He barely finished speaking when an icy finger ran down my neck. Sucking in a breath, my nipples hardened at the sudden shock of sensation.

"Are you well?" he asked.

"Yes, good, well," I managed.

A rumble of pleasure came from Zen as the bed sank near my legs. For a moment, I panicked about this bed frame sharing the same fate mine had, but The Crossroads had a very specific kind of clientele. Everything here was probably safe for Zen to use as he saw fit, stone or no.

"When I first beheld you on the rooftop, I thought your underthings ridiculously futile. These garments are somehow even more so." He chuckled as I felt a tug at the ribbon around my waist, the robe finally falling open.

Zen was quiet for a moment, pulling the lace off my shoulders and down my arms until the only contact I had with the robe was where I lay on it. A hand gently stroked my cheek, and I leaned into it. "The pink one has a keen eye for these garments."

"Tanya?" I asked. My body heated up, flushing at the uninhibited stare that scorched my body. Even though I couldn't see his gaze, I felt him taking in the red set Tanya insisted I wear. Another cold shock hit me; my nipple this time. Zen pressed an entire ice cube, dripping wet, against the bra. The lace, of course, did nothing to stop a freezing trail of water from rolling up my breast toward my neck, and I let out a panicked sound in surprise.

"Tell me how you feel," he urged.

"This is maddening," I panted, all the right parts of my body winding up with tension.

"I can stop if you want me to," Zen mused.

"Don't you *dare*—ah!" Burning hot, something roped around my leg high on my thigh.

*His tail.*

I felt the shift of weight on the mattress as Zen loomed over me, placing a kiss on the opposite breast.

"How did you get it so hot?" I asked.

Zen hummed. "The candles can heat more than the items on the table."

The tail that had circled my thigh was now withdrawing, and I focused on my breathing. My leg was still hot with the afterglow of it. His not-quite-stone skin wasn't sensitive to the temperature like mine was, and he could stand to hold any part of himself in either the ice or the fire for as long as he wanted. The thought sent a thrill through me.

"You enjoyed the heat, my stars?" Zen asked.

"Yes."

"May I try another source of heat?" he checked. "You need only tell me no, and I will withdraw."

"Do it," I said.

Sounds from the table had me wondering what was next, anticipation built with the thrumming of my pulse. A scalding drop of something hit my stomach. I groaned, turning it into an erotic sound as the sensual heat melted into my skin.

"Candle wax," Zen explained. "It contradicts what I know of humans and candles, but I was told these were made for this purpose."

"Yes, I've heard of it, but I've never seen one." Giving the sensation more thought, I reassured him. "*I like it.*"

Zen dripped wax on my collarbone, then my thigh, before catching me off guard by setting an ice cube on my sternum, right between my breasts. He must have set the wax aside, because no more stings of hot and cold touched my skin as Zen began kissing a trail from my lips to my neck, then lifting my upper half. Unclasping the bra, the ice he had placed between my breasts slid down my side and landed on the bed, where Zen picked it up and tossed it back into the bowl. He pulled the lace from me, leaving only the panties that did little to cover much of anything.

I could feel Zen playing with my left nipple, taking the other into his mouth. With a moan, I clutched at the bed sheets for want of something to hold on to while he turned his attentions from one side to the other.

"Zen," I let out, breathless. "That feels so good, but I want something *in* me." A veritable truth, bolting from my mouth with the sheer desperation I felt building. I pressed my thighs together, shifting my hips and desperately trying to find friction to satisfy my empty, clenching core..

"Soon, my stars," Zen said as he pulled away from my breasts, leaving behind peaked nipples and my heavy pants of desperation.

Before I could take his words into consideration, Zen slid my panties aside in another swift motion before something solid and burning pressed against my clit.

"What is that?" I squealed as my body tried to pull away from it. But Zen held me in place, imposing his sensual tortures upon me.

"Tell me if it becomes unbearable and I will remove it at once." His non-answer was of no assurance to me as he swirled the hard heat around my clit, eliciting more sounds of desperation from me. He moved the firm object down, swirling it through the need pooling at my entrance as he played, barely dipping in and out of me. It quickly became so fucking frustrating that I couldn't stand it anymore.

"Please, Zen, I need something in me *now*!"

"As you wish." One side of the panties ripped, and I found myself momentarily surprised that they'd lasted this long. As the useless threads fell out of the way, that hot, smooth whatever-he-had slid down again until it rubbed against a very different entrance. Sucking in a breath, I stilled.

Zen waited, probably to see if I would object, and when I didn't, he slid it inside as slowly as he could. The pressure built until the firm object popped in, lodged firmly in place. I'd never experienced this before, and as I adjusted to the feeling, I decided that I didn't hate it, but I was glad it wasn't very big.

My gargoyle didn't stop there. I soon found out what the metal things in the dish were, causing me to regret that I hadn't paid much attention to them before I was blindfolded as two ice-cold clamps pinched my nipples. A gasp escaped, turning into a whine as *hot* fingers worked my clit.

"Zen," I groaned.

"Yes, my stars?" he murmured, teasing a finger in and out of my entrance as I squirmed.

"If you don't get this stuff off of me and fuck me right now, I'm going to rip this blindfold off and take care of myself without you," I threatened, fully at my limit.

His hand withdrew as he laughed. Then he removed everything from my body, except for the butt plug. I felt something thick and hard pressed against me as he warmly said, "As you wish, my feisty human."

The blindfold came off with gentle hands, and the first thing I saw was Zen's smile. My body relaxed, and I reached to pull his face down for a kiss. Zen eased onto the bed, lifting me completely. As he leaned against the headboard, he placed me on his lap, his hands at my waist, positioning me even as we kept stealing kisses.

"Spread your thighs wider for me, my stars," Zen rumbled, tugging at my earlobe with his teeth. I did as I was told, and my reward was to feel his hard tip pressed to my slick entrance.

"This is what you desire?" he asked. I tried to wiggle down onto him, but he held his arms up just enough that I couldn't.

"Yes, no teasing!" I pleaded. And in one motion, he speared me on his cock. My head fell back as my breath left me for a moment, the fullness of him leaving me breathless.

Zen pulled our bodies close, peppering kisses across my shoulders and breasts. "I could spend an eternity kissing every star on your skin," he murmured.

His hands began a desperate dance, lifting me to pull out of me, before rushing me back down on his cock again. Any movement I contributed was almost an afterthought as the gargoyle beneath me bounced me up and down, winding us both higher and higher. Fevered kisses and desperate hands roamed freely.

"I'm not going to last," I admitted between hot, quick breaths. So full, there wasn't a movement Zen could make that didn't have him rubbing me in all the right places. He growled, a pleased sound rumbling through him as he bounced me on his cock.

"Give it to me, Henri," he commanded. "Show me the beautiful face of my human when she's been satisfied by her gargoyle."

*Her gargoyle. My gargoyle.* He was mine as much as I was his, and for lack of anything to hold on to, I flung my arms around his neck and cried out my release. Zen didn't stop heaving me onto him as muscles clenched and heat flared, forcing me to ride the waves of orgasm all the way to the bottom as I crashed against him. Zen roared, his own release overflowing from my body onto the tousled sheets.

Both of us spent, he laid me back on the bed, keeping my knees apart as his hungry gaze ate up the sight before him. I lay there and allowed him to bask in the moment, too tired from a long day of panic and worry and mindboggling sex.

"Would if I could have you this way at the end of every night," he murmured.

The image flooded my mind with a shiver. "Are you sure you prefer your rooftop to staying in the apartment with me?"

He was quiet a moment, weighing the words. I had asked him a long time ago, when our relationship was newer and less sure. But if he changed his mind, I would be happy to have him safely under my roof when the sun was out and he was in his most vulnerable state. If anything, the landlord would just think he was another one of my projects.

Zen got off the bed, retrieving the towels from the table as he began to clean up the mess we'd made of ourselves and the bed.

"Henri of Crossgate, I would be honored to dwell with you. I vow to keep you safe, fed, and satisfied for as long as you will have me."

I may not have had much energy left, but I had enough to get up on my knees and pull my gargoyle into a hug. "All I need is you, Zen. And I promise to watch over you during the day, and help you with whatever you need from the city, and to stay by your side."

Zen lifted me, spinning us around the room. "It is a deal, my stars. I will be with you always."

# Chapter Twenty-Eight

## Henri

"I'm so nervous," I said for the hundredth time, standing between Chloe and Simon in the cool fall air. The trees in Riverview Park were aflame in oranges, reds, and yellows, with most of the walking paths taken up by scarf-clad observers walking through the contest's submitted statues. Journalists spread out amongst the observers, and the judges deliberated in their tent off to the side. Chloe had an arm looped through mine as we both held coffees, attempting to keep the chill from our fingers.

"It will be fine," Simon promised, rubbing my back. "You'll either win, or you won't."

"I wanted the prize money," I groaned before taking a sip of my drink.

"You've been selling a lot more pieces at Magical Muse lately, haven't you?" Chloe asked.

With a shrug, I looked down the path where my sculpture stood. With the appearance of an ornate picture frame, the only thing in it was the twists and turns of the river that ran through the city. I'd left the stone thick enough that I didn't think it would break easily, but you could see all the way through it with a view of the skyline in the distance. My vision for the piece came out just how I wanted it to, with a few months of work and several trial runs. After making half a dozen smaller frames for practice, Rita started selling them at the shop and they moved surprisingly well. A florist wanted three for displays in his store, and private collectors grabbed the rest. It wasn't a huge leap to start carving small-scale versions of the gothic architectural details I loved so much, and they were more than keeping me afloat now.

"There's my girl!" Speak of the devil, Rita rounded the path in a lemon-yellow quilted peacoat and rainbow knit cap. She thrust her arms out toward my sculpture in animated astonishment. "That's the best thing I've seen in ages!"

"Right?" Simon chimed in. "If she doesn't win, those judges have no taste."

"Stop it," I elbowed him. "There are a bunch of amazing pieces here."

"And yours is the best one," Chloe agreed, smiling over at Simon. I could feel them reach around behind me to hold hands.

"Okay, that's about enough of that." I stepped forward, turning in time to see them move closer, Chloe's head resting on Simon's shoulder. "I love you two lovebirds, but hold hands without me between you."

Simon rolled his eyes, and Chloe busied herself with a long draw from her cup.

"Is that Omari?" Rita asked, smacking her forehead. "I knew the vibes of that fountain one were familiar! Sorry kids, I have to go see an old friend. Good luck, Henri!"

"Thanks," I said, waving her off as she strode down the path to one of the other artists.

Taking a drink, my eyes drifted to the skyline where Old Town would sit. I couldn't see them from here, but I knew there were a dozen gargoyles pointed in this direction, just waiting for the sun to finish dipping down below the horizon so they could come alive and hear the results of the competition. Smiling into my cup, my cheeks flushed at the image of Zen trying to keep my mind from my anxiety last night.

"Earth to Henri," Chloe teased. "What was that about lovebirds?"

"Shut up," I said, eliciting laughter from both of them, which became infectious enough to pull me in as well.

We waited a bit longer as I kept eyeing the judging tent and biting the inside of my cheek. Finishing my coffee, I excused myself from the gooey-eyed couple I'd brought with me and walked over to dispose of the cup. I just made it to the bin when a pair of long legs in a gray pantsuit came into view, standing right beside me. Startling, I lifted my head and found Harriet standing to my left.

"Hello, Henri," she offered. Her hair was as impeccably styled as ever, her suit tidy and free of wrinkles with long expensive-looking scarf draped around her neck. She carried a hot drink in a gloved hand.

*Put together as always, sis.*

I eyed the office building nearby where my family's law firm would have the perfect view of the action. "If you're bothered by the crowd, it will be gone soon."

"No. No, I . . ." Harriet sighed, finishing her drink and putting the cup in the same bin I had. "I wanted to come out to support you."

My eyebrows pinched together. "What?"

She pulled a folded piece of paper from her pocket and handed it to me. I opened up a flyer for the centennial competition as she spoke. "I wanted to apologize about the last time we bumped into each other. I knew you must be one of the entries." She took a brief look around before circling back to me. "They're all so beautiful. It's good work, and I wanted to tell you that."

I didn't know what to say to her when we weren't bickering, so I just folded my arms under my chest for warmth and nodded. Looking over my shoulder, I found Chloe and Simon watching me curiously.

"Look," I sighed. "I really appreciate you coming down to say something. I'm sorry about how things happened last time, too."

She smiled. "It's okay. I was a bit of an ass."

I snorted. "And I could have handled it better."

Harriet hummed, her eyes roaming over the statues. "So, which one is yours?"

Pointing, I took a few steps down the sidewalk to show her a clearer view of it. She stood for a long moment, taking it in before turning back to me.

"It's lovely. I hope you win, and I wish you the best of luck, Henri."

My eyebrows jumped at the use of my preferred name, but it also brought a genuine smile to my lips. "Thanks."

She shivered. "I'm going to head back up to the office before my nose falls off. I can't believe it's already getting this cold."

"You never could handle it," I teased. "Alright, see you later, Harriet."

She smiled and took a few steps, but then paused and turned around. "Um, if it's alright with you, would you text me sometime? I'd like to get lunch and catch up. I'm playing again."

"Playing . . . the violin?" My mouth popped open.

She nodded, her cheeks flushing. "Every other Sunday, with two friends at a cafe."

*And if Harriet can try this hard to meet me in the middle, I can do the same.*

"I'd like that," I offered. "I'll text you."

She grinned and gave me a nod. "Okay, I'm really going this time. I have some documents I need to go over before the end of the day."

"Alright, later." Watching her go, I walked back over to Simon and Chloe.

"Was that—" Chloe started, but the sound of the judges exiting their tents cut her off., We soberly watched as they made their way to the empty platform where the winning statue would eventually take center place.

"Thank you all for coming!" an older man in a suit-jacket announced into a microphone, drawing a hush over the crowd as artists and onlookers alike gave him their full attention. He had some speech prepared, reading from a card in his hand occasionally, but mostly going on about the centennial of the city while I died inside waiting for the announcement.

"If you tap your foot any harder, you're going to rub the soles right off your boot," Simon teased.

"Be nice," Chloe hissed, poking him in the arm.

I didn't even say anything snarky in reply. I could only stay laser-focused on the man at the platform.

"After deliberating—"

"This is it!" Chloe whispered.

"Our winning sculpture, and the piece that will decorate Riverview Park, is . . ."

The door creaked as it fell shut behind me. Even though the sun fell behind the horizon on my walk from the bus stop, my apartment was warmly lit and cozy. A fire crackled in the fireplace, and Zen was slicing up potatoes on the cutting board. He put down the knife and strode over to me, lifting me in his arms.

"There you are, my stars!" He spun us in a circle before putting me back down on my feet. "You must tell me everything. How was the competition? Did you defeat your enemies?"

Giving him a tight smile, I shrugged off my scarf and tossed it toward the coat rack. "There were no enemies to defeat, Zen. It's a contest, not a fight to the death."

Zen frowned. "Still, you must tell me what happened. If only the event did not happen during the day," he growled.

"It's okay. There isn't anything we could have done about it." I shrugged.

Zen's head snapped to the window. "The others, we must tell them."

He scooped me into his arms, striding across the room as I protested. Pushing open the window, he pulled me in tight and leapt.

My fear of heights was still there, but much tamer now than it was after the fearful day when Havaxus carried me off in the rain. Thankfully, Zen didn't have to go farther than the next rooftop over, where he used to spend his days.

We landed, and seven gargoyles descended on us.

"Were you victorious, my matron?" Marzav asked.

"I told you not to call me that," I said.

"You are the mate of Zendrax. That makes you our matron," the old scoundrel countered with a smile.

"Will your trophy be displayed for all to see?" Kana, a younger female with dark wings, practically bounced as she asked.

"Tell us of your victory," Haltsap, a more seasoned warrior, asked from the back.

"Silence!" Zendrax held up a hand. "Allow Henri to speak, if you wish to know the outcome."

He turned to me, wings half-shielding me from the breeze, with a smile that could melt me right into his arms. But I folded my arms, offering no smile in return as I tilted my head down.

Zen sucked in a breath, then put a hand on each of my shoulders. "Oh, my stars."

"I won!" I screamed, and the gargoyles exploded in riotous cheers.

Zen lifted me, and I clung to him just in time for him to fall off the edge of the roof to catch the wind currents. Marzav and the rest followed behind until we were a parade of gargoyles slipping up into the obscuring clouds.

"Where are we going?" I laughed.

"To the mountains!" Zen offered, leaning down to kiss me. "We must tell the clan."

Laughing, I buried my face into Zen's chest as he swept us away for my victory lap to where the bulk of the gargoyles made their home. Me, my gargoyle, and the life I wouldn't trade for anything in the world.

My home.

# Thank You For Reading!

I hope you enjoyed Zendrax & Henri's story ♥

Thank you for taking a chance on my book.

If you enjoyed this story, please leave your honest reviews on

Amazon, Goodreads,

or on any of your social media platforms!

**Hungry for more reads?**

Explore Sabrina Blackburry's backlist, be the first to

know about upcoming releases, sneak peeks, and more at

Sabrinablackburry.com

Thank you for being part of this journey—you're amazing!

# Acknowledgments

There are a lot of moving parts to publishing a book. I have been blessed by the team at Wattpad Books with my debut book and series, so I knew undertaking my first self-published book would be a difficult road. Many people deserve thanks for their help along the way, and I want to address them here.

To the other Monsters of Crossgate authors, Reina Frost and Eden Hale, I quite literally would not have done this without you. There are no two other authors I would want to create a monster romance setting with, I can't wait to see how our combined imaginations shape this setting.

To the ones who helped me with the parts I could not do myself. My cover artist KitFoxArt, thank you for the beautiful work. To my editor Ashley Wessel, thank you for the edits and the many amusing comments you left, it made the job much more enjoyable. To my formatter, Lashell Rain, I would have been so lost without you.

To the ones who stayed with me when it was only a work in progress. To the Monsters of Crossgate beta readers, I love you all very much and you are truly a special part of my day. Thank you. And to my street team and ARC readers, I am so thankful for each of you and all you've done to help me spread the word of this release.

To my family and friends, thank you for your support. Thank you to Act II Butter Lovers popcorn, without you I probably would not have eaten during many writing sessions.

And last but not least, as I mentioned in the dedication, thank you to Keith David. You know what you did. My monster-lover era began with Goliath. Thank you for your part in starting me down this path (I think).

# About the author

Sabrina Blackburry lives a quiet life in central Missouri with her husband and son. She enjoys walking nature trails, playing tabletop games, visiting coffee shops, and participating in the local renaissance festival. Raised by her grandparents who are now gone, she maintains a close relationship with her mother and three sisters. She credits her grandfather's imagination for the birth of her storytelling.

With an early passion for fantasy and books, she began writing seriously in her twenties leading to her debut novel Dirty Lying Faeries in 2022. Always with fantasy elements, her books focus on characters finding their place in the world, and telling stories of love with a touch of magic. Sabrina's favorite part of writing is filling the meat of the story with side characters that can enhance the plot and main characters. She believes when a character is never wholly good or evil, that is when they can flourish.

"I believe that the best stories are the ones that make you forget where you are for a little while. If all I manage to do in my career is make a few readers smile, I'll have accomplished my dreams."

www.ingramcontent.com/pod-product-compliance
Lightning Source LLC
Chambersburg PA
CBHW020558180626
46810CB00007B/2562